'Mr Cavaletti—or Dr Cavaletti—whichever you prefer,' Rachel said, trying hard to sound icily in control while in reality the smile and shoulder shrug had turned her bones to jelly.

'Just because Kurt isn't my boyfriend it doesn't mean I don't have one. I don't know how you do things back in Italy, but you're moving far too fast.'

'I'm sorry, but I felt an attraction.' He offered an apologetic smile. 'I'm not normally impulsive.'

Shoot—the man's remorse was nearly as good as his smile!

'You *do* have a boyfriend?'

Rachel stared at him. The lie—a simple yes—hovered on the tip of her tongue. An easy word to say—a single syllable—but she'd left it too late, because he was smiling again.

Then he leaned forward and kissed her, first on one cheek, then on the other, and while Rachel pressed her hands to her burning cheeks he walked away.

JIMMIE'S CHILDREN'S UNIT

*The Children's Cardiac Unit,
St James's Hospital, Sydney. A specialist unit
where the dedicated staff mend children's hearts...
and their own!*

**JIMMIE'S CHILDREN'S UNIT
...where hearts are mended!**

THE ITALIAN SURGEON

BY
MEREDITH WEBBER

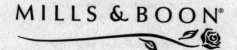

MILLS & BOON®

First published in Great Britain 2005
Harlequin Mills & Boon Limited,
Eton House, 18-24 Paradise Road, Richmond, Surrey TW9 1SR

© Meredith Webber 2005

ISBN 0 263 84330 0

Set in Times Roman 10½ on 12 pt.
03-0905-44965

Printed and bound in Spain
by Litografía Rosés, S.A., Barcelona

CHAPTER ONE

RACHEL dropped her mask and gown into the bin as she walked out of the operating theatre. Too tired to be bothered showering and changing immediately, she headed straight for the small theatre lounge, where she slumped down into an armchair and pulled off her cap.

'I think it is close to criminal that such beautiful hair should be hidden under such an ugly cap,' a deep, accented voice remarked, and Rachel, her fingers threaded through the hair in question, turned in alarm.

The voice certainly didn't belong to any of the members of the paediatric cardiac surgical team here at Jimmie's—she'd all but lived with them for the past year, at first in Melbourne, where the team had spent six months, and since then in Sydney!

The body didn't belong to anyone on the team either—here was a serious hunk, not overly tall, but solid in a way that would make any woman want to experience being held in his arms.

This was a dispassionate observation—made on behalf of all womankind—not personal at all. She no longer did personal observations of men.

Now an ultra-white smile flashed from the kind of face Rachel had only ever seen in ads for men's fashion—expensive men's fashion. But this was no photographic image—this was drop-dead handsome in real life.

She suspected her observation was becoming a tad less dispassionate, and was puzzled by it.

Dark eyes, set beneath ebony brows, met hers.

'You don't know me. I was late arriving—too late for introductions. I am Luca Cavaletti, here to observe and learn from Alex and all his team.'

He smiled again, then added, 'Including you.'

Bemused by some very unaccustomed physical reactions to a man, she could only stare at him, though she did clench her fingers, which desperately wanted to move to her head again and fluff up the hat-hair she knew was on show. Hat-hair tousled into knots by her fingers' initial foray through it.

'You were in Theatre?' she asked, her eyes, fascinated by his strongly boned face, strayed to clearly delineated lips then moved back to study the dark, piercing eyes.

Crikey, it was as if she'd never seen a man before!

Thanks to a show she'd watched on TV back home in the States, 'Crikey' was about the only 'Australianism' she'd known before she'd come down under with Alex and the team, and she used it in her thoughts all the time.

'I thought it seemed a little more crowded than usual, though Alex and Phil always draw a number of onlookers.'

'Ah, but I'm more a student than an onlooker. I'm a qualified paediatric cardiac surgeon, but Alex has techniques we don't use in Italy, and the whole team has a cohesiveness that is known throughout the world. I'm fortunate enough to be here for four weeks,' the man said, taking the chair across from Rachel so she was no longer looking up at him.

Maybe from this new angle her hair didn't look quite as bad!

Maybe she should have a brain transplant to stop this reaction thing happening.

She let her fingers escape for one quick ruffle at the front, and tried to remember what Alex had said about someone coming to observe for a few weeks.

Someone fabulously wealthy! She stole another glance at the man, though she doubted she could tell a rich man from a poor one just by looking, especially if both were in that great leveller—theatre pyjamas!

'There's coffee in the pot over there and sandwiches in the refrigerator,' she said, not because she felt obliged to play hostess but because she was back to cataloguing the stranger's physical attributes and couldn't think of anything else to say.

And she'd found a flaw—a slight scar running across his left eyebrow, marring the perfect symmetry of that feature but adding to, rather than detracting from, his beauty. No, beauty was far too feminine a word when this man was masculinity personified.

She touched her own scar, a far more jagged and less appealing mark, running down her hairline from left temple to left ear, the result not of anything dramatic but of falling off her bicycle onto broken glass when she'd been five. Then, thinking again of the man's good looks, she smiled to herself, wondering what Kurt would make of him.

'Can I pour you a coffee?' he asked.

And sit here in theatre scrubs, no make-up and impossible hair while the archetypical Latin lover was sitting opposite her?

She might not be interested in men, but as a woman she had some pride!

'No, thanks, I need to grab a shower and change. I just came in to sit down for a little while to gather up the energy to make the next move.'

'Of course, of all the team, you have the longest time in Theatre—seeing everything is ready first, then assisting the surgeon who makes the primary incision and prepares the heart for Alex, as well as assisting him. With the added tension of operating on such tiny infants, you must be exhausted by the finish.'

Seduced more by the understanding in his words than by the soft accent that curled around them, Rachel smiled.

'I don't think the tension I feel is nearly as bad as the stress the surgeons are under,' she said. 'Yes, I have more theatre time, but my job is the easy one.'

He shook his head and smiled, as if he knew better, but then he turned away, apparently taking up her offer of a coffee. She struggled to her feet, told them to walk, not run, and left the room, escaping to the washrooms where, if necessary, she could resort to the time-honoured convention of a cold shower.

Though wasn't it men who usually needed cold showers?

And, physiologically, why would they work?

Did blood really heat in a sexual reaction to another person?

It certainly wasn't a topic she remembered covering in nursing school.

And she couldn't possibly be having a sexual re-action to the man, anyway. No way! He was another colleague, nothing more. And his charm was probably as natural to him as breathing.

What had he said his name was? Luca—she re-

membered that part, because the way he'd said it had
lilted off his tongue.

What would he make of Rachel?

How would her name sound, whispered in that
husky accent?

She banged her head against the wall of the shower
stall. Kurt was right. She really should get out more.

'You OK in there?'

Maggie's voice.

'I'm fine, just bumped against the wall,' Rachel
lied, but hearing Maggie reminded her she *was* going
to get out more—starting tonight! Maggie and Phil's
engagement party at the Italian restaurant not far from
the hospital—a restaurant the whole team now fre-
quented.

But going out to eat with other members of the
team—even attending an engagement party—did not
constitute 'getting out more', Rachel reminded herself. Getting out more, in Kurt's view, meant dating—
going out with a man, perhaps having a relationship.

She shuddered at the thought, and felt a suggestion
of old pain, like a hidden bruise, somewhere deep
within her, but then an image of the Italian's face
flashed up in her mind's eye, and the shudder became
a shiver…

She showered—under hot water, damn the cold—
dried herself and dressed, hoping she wouldn't run
into tall, dark and deadly again because she'd woken
late this morning and dragged on the first clothes
she'd put her hands on—a pair of comfy but far from
young sweat pants, and a bulky, misshapen sweater
her mother, during a knitting phase of her exploration
of various handicrafts, had knitted for her.

Knitted with more love than skill—the love ingredient ensuring Rachel had worn it to death.

She poked her head out of the shower stall. The changing room was used by both male and female members of the team, and she usually checked she wasn't going to embarrass anyone before emerging.

The unspoken but commonly agreed standard of embarrassment was total nudity. Underwear was OK, though the thought of seeing Luca whoever-he-was in tight black briefs made Rachel's mouth go dry.

The reality of him in that identical garb had her reaching for the door of the shower stall for support.

Kurt was definitely right about her getting out more, though the thought made her heart quail and again the remembered pain pressed against her ribs.

Perhaps she could just date. Go out with a guy a couple of times—really casual—enough to get used to being around a man again.

Though she worked with men all the time, so it wasn't lack of male companionship that had her reacting the way she was to the temporary team member.

'You are finished in the shower?'

She opened her mouth and formed her lips to say the word, but whether a 'yes' came out she wasn't sure. None of the other team members had olive skin stretched tight across their chests—skin that clung lovingly to flat slabs of muscle.

Well, not that she'd noticed, anyway...

'Talk about buffed!' Kurt whispered in her ear, appearing from nowhere, taking her arm and guiding her across the room to the washbasins and mirrors. 'The man is gorgeous, but I'm pretty sure he's all yours.

No signals at all in my direction, and I'm not wearing my very worst clothes.'

'You know I don't care!' she snapped at Kurt. 'I couldn't be less interested.'

But in spite of her defiant words, Rachel glanced down at her unglamorous attire and winced, then looked up at herself in the mirror and groaned.

'In any case, there's no way a man like him— Didn't Alex say something about him being rich and famous? Famous in his own country?'

She didn't wait for Kurt's nod, but continued, 'Well, a man like that wouldn't be interested in a woman like me, even at the best of times. But today?' She smiled at Kurt. 'I think we both miss out. Anyway he was probably snapped up years ago. Married with two point five children would be my guess.'

'He's not.'

Rachel stared at her friend's reflection.

'Not what?'

'Not married. No ring. Continental men were into wearing wedding rings long before we Americans adopted the custom.'

'But no one wears a ring in Theatre, so you can't tell.'

Kurt sighed, as he often did when he was shown what he called the depth of her ignorance of the male sex.

'The guy's got naturally olive skin, but he's tanned as well—babies aren't born that delectable bronze colour. And there's no pale mark around his finger where a ring has been.'

Rachel poked her tongue at him.

'Smart-ass!' she said, but her silly heart was skipping with excitement as she dragged a comb through her wet hair. A whole string of 'crikeys' echoed in her head, the only possible means of expressing the disbelief she felt about this situation.

Here she was reacting to a man as if she were a teenager—she, who hadn't been interested in a man for years. True, from time to time she tried to pretend, mainly when well-meaning friends threw men at her, but none of them had ever sparked the slightest physical response or filled her with an urge to get involved again.

In fact, the thought of getting involved again made her stomach clench.

'Damn this hair. It's impossible to manage. I shouldn't have let you talk me into growing it.'

Kurt took the comb from her hand and carefully drew it through the tangled curls.

'It's beautiful hair,' he reminded her. 'So beautiful it was a sin to keep it cropped short purely for convenience. Besides, as I pointed out to you when we first came to Australia, how would you have known a good hairdresser from a bad one? And for short hair you need the best. Far better to have grown it.'

Finished, he handed back the comb, while, behind them, Luca emerged from the shower, this time with a snowy white towel draped around his hips. It didn't do anything to diminish his good looks!

He came towards the mirror, nodding to Kurt who had hurried to grab the shower before someone else went in. With only two stalls, the competition among the team was usually fierce.

'You and Kurt are a couple?'

Still conversing in the mirror rather than face to face, Rachel saw herself as well as the dark-featured man. So she also saw the frown that drew her eye-brows together, and the look of puzzlement in her own eyes.

'Me and Kurt? No.'

Not knowing why he was asking—he couldn't possibly be interested in her as they'd barely met—she wasn't prepared to offer any more information. She tucked her comb into her toiletry bag and carried it over to her locker, pleased to have a reason to move away from the double whammy of the man and his mirror image.

'Good,' he said, following her and holding open her locker door. Far too much bronzed skin, now Kurt had drawn her attention to it, far too close to her body.

'So perhaps there is someone else in your life?'

'Are you coming on to me?' Rachel demanded, more angered by her reaction to his presence than by the pace of his approach. 'Why? Because I'm convenient? Save you looking elsewhere for someone to while away the off-duty hours for the time you're here?'

She grabbed the door of her locker away from him and slammed it shut, then remembered she needed to get her shoulder-bag out and had to open it again.

Luca whoever was staring at her with a puzzled expression in his so-dark eyes.

'I'm sorry. I've offended you.' His accent was more marked now, and he did sound genuinely regretful. 'But I know Maggie and Phil are a couple, and Annie and Alex also. I thought perhaps you and Kurt…'

He held out his hands in a typical Mediterranean gesture.

'Not in this world, or the next, though I love the

woman dearly.' Kurt, who must have heard the conversation, smirked as he sashayed past them.

What was it with these men that they were in and out of the shower so quickly?

And what had got into Kurt that he was talking and joking this way? Kurt the silent was how most people thought of him, though Rachel knew him better and understood why he usually listened more than he talked.

Loud conversation signalled the arrival of more members of the team: Alex Attwood, team leader and top paediatric cardiac surgeon; Phil Park who was all but through a five-year fellowship with Alex; and Scott Douglas, the surgical registrar here at St James's Hospital, who was currently on roster with their team.

'Ah, Luca, you've met these two indispensable members of my crew,' Alex said, coming towards them. 'Rachel, as you no doubt saw, is the best physician's assistant any surgeon could ever have, while Kurt's refinements to the heart-lung bypass machine have made operating on neonates far safer for the patient and far easier for me.'

Luca put out his hand to acknowledge Alex's introduction to Kurt, then turned, hand still extended, to Rachel.

'We've not been formally introduced,' he said to Alex, but his eyes were on Rachel, and though she was reasonably sure eyes couldn't send subliminal messages, she was certainly receiving something that made her feel tingly all over, even before his hand engulfed hers, and strong, warm fingers applied gentle pressure.

'Luca Cavaletti.'

He released her hand but his eyes still held hers.

By this time Rachel was so thoroughly confused by her physical reactions to him, her mind had stopped working.

Or almost stopped working...

'Rachel Lerini,' she managed to respond, and wasn't surprised when the man to whom she'd spoken let fly in a stream of Italian.

'Whoa there!' she said, recovering enough composure to hold up her hand. 'My great-grandfather brought the name to America and while it's been passed on, his language certainly wasn't. *Ciao, prego* and pasta—that's the limit of my Italian.'

'Perhaps I will have time to teach you new words,' he said softly.

Rachel frowned at him. She hadn't totally forgotten how things worked between men and women in the dating game and from what she remembered, this man was moving far too fast for her to feel comfortable.

Actually, her physical reactions—silly things like tingles and shivers—were making her more wary, rather than more attracted. It was so weird.

So unlike anything she'd experienced before...

So new...

She was so busy trying to work out what was happening, she didn't realise the man was still there—and talking to her!

'Are you already going with someone or would you like to be my date tonight at the party?'

'No.'

The word positively erupted from her lips, so blunt it sounded rude. Politeness forced her to explain, 'It's not that kind of party. It's a celebration for Phil and Maggie, and a double celebration in a way because some bad stuff that's been happening for the team has been resolved. But it's a team party—everyone goes—so you don't need a date.'

'Besides, if she did need a date, she's got me,' Kurt said, turning from the washbasin a little distance away where he'd been pretending to wash out a small bottle while listening avidly to the conversation.

'She's the cat's mother!' Rachel spat the words at her well-meaning friend. She definitely wanted to fend Luca off—to slow him down—but she wasn't altogether, one hundred per cent, absolutely and utterly certain that she wanted to lose his attention altogether.

And *that* thought was even scarier than her physical reactions. Crikey—it was hard to know what she wanted.

Though given that it had been months since she'd had even a casual date, and four years since her marriage had ended in the most disastrous way possible, maybe a four-week flirtation with Luca Cavaletti might be just what the doctor ordered.

The person inside her head groaned at the weak pun.

'I'm going to the office to do some paperwork,' Rachel said, hoping the Italian would take the hint and move away to torment someone else. 'I'll see you at home, Kurt.'

She walked away, but escape was never going to be that easy. Stopping outside the changing room to talk to Annie, who was checking the lists for the following day, meant Luca caught up with her and then accompanied her to the suite of rooms the team used for an office.

'You live with Kurt?' he said, following her into

the room, his voice alerting Becky, the secretary, who was manning the front desk.

'Yes.'

'But he flirts with me! He's gay, isn't he?'

Rachel wasn't sure if he was being sexist or not, but years of defending Kurt, her best friend, had her hackles rising.

'So?' she demanded, and Luca's smile lit up his face as he stretched his arms wide to each side and shrugged his broad shoulders.

'So he's not your boyfriend, just your friend,' he said, then he turned and winked at Becky who was staring at the two of them as if this was a show put on solely for her amusement.

'Mr Cavaletti—or Dr Cavaletti—whichever you prefer,' Rachel said, trying hard to sound icily in control while in reality the smile and shrug had turned her bones to jelly and she was considering returning to the shower to try the cold-water treatment. 'Just because Kurt isn't my boyfriend, it doesn't mean I don't have one. I don't know how you do things back in Italy, but for an American woman, you're moving far too fast. If you're anxious about the limited time you have here in Australia, then go sweep someone else off her feet. Mine are staying firmly on the ground.'

'I'm sorry, but I felt an attraction—the hair maybe—I don't know…' He offered an apologetic smile. 'I'm not normally impulsive.'

Shoot—it was with difficulty she stifled the 'crikey'—but the man's remorse was nearly as good as his smile! The feet, which she'd said were firmly planted, now seemed to be floating several inches above the floor.

Luca touched her lightly on the shoulder.

'You *do* have a boyfriend?'

Rachel stared at him. Big opportunity here! The lie—a simple yes—hovered on the tip of her tongue. An easy word to say—a single syllable—but she'd left it too late, because he was smiling again.

'I will slow down!' he said softly.

Then he leaned forward and kissed her, first on one cheek, then on the other. And while Rachel pressed her hands to the burning patches of skin, he walked away.

'If you don't want him, give him to me,' Becky said, her awed tone conveying loads more than the words themselves.

'Feel free,' Rachel told her, but Becky shook her head.

'It seems he's only got eyes for you.'

Embarrassed, both by Becky's words and the little pantomime that had been played out in front of the secretary, Rachel shook her head in denial.

'It's the hair,' she told Becky. 'Apparently it's not a common colour in Italy.'

'It is beautiful, your hair,' Becky told her. 'A true red-gold. Makes us blondes look ordinary.' She eyed Rachel consideringly before adding, 'Although I'd always been given to understand Italian men went for blondes. What are you wearing tonight?'

The question was so transparent Rachel laughed.

'My old flannel pyjamas with Snoopy all over them?' she teased.

'That might work,' Becky said, 'though if he's hooked on your hair he probably wouldn't notice anything else. Pity, because Alex was saying he's rich as well as gorgeous—well, Alex didn't say he was gorgeous, that was me.'

Rachel chuckled and headed for the desk she shared with Kurt. So Luca *was* the wealthy man Alex had mentioned.

And with looks and money, he was probably used to women falling at his feet, when he went into flirt mode.

Well, if he was expecting her to fall anywhere near his feet tonight, whatever she was wearing, he was in for a disappointment!

Ignoring a twinge of regret she didn't want to analyse, Rachel turned her attention back to work. She wanted to check on the paperwork from today's operation—make sure all the team members present had signed it—then look at the programme for the following week. Alex had suggested she take some time off, but she didn't want to leave him with a new assistant for any complex cases.

Tonight could wait…

CHAPTER TWO

SHE wore black. A slinky silk jersey dress Kurt had talked her into spending an entire pay cheque on when the team had been working in Melbourne. She'd worn it to Alex's wedding to Annie, the team's manager, and would probably have to wear it again when Phil and Maggie, the team anaesthetist, were married, as she certainly didn't want to splash out on another expensive outfit.

'No one will recognise it as the same dress,' Kurt assured her as they walked the short distance to the restaurant. 'The wedding was in the afternoon, and you wore it with a white jacket and those divine white and black sandals. Tonight it's pure sex appeal.'

Then, without giving Rachel time to protest, he added, 'Though my guess is you could be wearing your Snoopy pyjamas for all the attention the Italian will give to your clothes.'

'Ho!' Rachel scoffed, but just thinking about Luca brought butterflies to her stomach, and she wondered how she was going to get through the evening.

And why, after all this time, she was feeling such strong physical reactions to a man...

'That is a beautiful dress, but no more beautiful than the woman wearing it,' Luca, standing outside the restaurant as if expecting her arrival, greeted her.

'That kind of over-the-top compliment might be flattering to an Italian woman,' Rachel told him, cross because now her heart was racing and, with the butterflies fluttering wildly, internally she was a mess. 'But American women are more embarrassed than flattered by people saying things like that.'

'Is that so?' Luca responded, quite matter-of-factly, as if she hadn't been deliberately rude to him. 'Then, as well as slowing down, I must tone down my compliments, although they're no less genuine for being—what did you call it?—over the top?'

He took her arm and led her up the stairs. Kurt, who'd walked ahead when they'd reached Luca, was watching from the top with a grin of teasing delight. Rachel glared at her best friend, though she knew he wasn't the cause of her consternation, because in spite of her denial she was, in some peculiar way, both flattered by Luca's compliments and excited by his company.

And his touch...

No way! She was definitely not going there!

Dating was one thing, but a relationship?

Though if he was only here for four weeks...

She drew away from him, unable to believe the way her mind was working. How could she even consider such a thing? Especially with a man like this—so far out of her league they were practically different species.

Maggie and Phil were waiting just inside, Maggie reaching out to take Rachel's hand and draw her close for a kiss.

'If I wasn't so besotted by Phil, I'd be throwing myself at that man,' she whispered to Rachel. 'Isn't he gorgeous?'

'I guess so.' The reluctant admission was forced from Rachel's lips, making Maggie laugh. Rachel moved on, kissed Phil and offered her congratulations once again, then Kurt was by her side, leading her to a table on the far side of the room.

'Thought you might have needed a breather from that walking sex god,' he said, and Rachel nodded, thinking if she stayed away from Luca, the butterflies might settle enough to make room for food in her stomach.

It might also give her mind time to sort out what was happening, and remember all the reasons she no longer did relationships.

With *any* man!

But avoiding Luca was like avoiding Aussie flies in summer. Impossible. The meal was no sooner finished than he appeared by her chair.

'You will dance with me?'

Maggie and Phil were already on the dance floor, and a number of the nursing staff and their partners had joined them. Rachel glanced at Kurt who offered no help at all, announcing he and Becky were going to show the team how real dancers danced.

Rachel stood up, then realised immediately how big a mistake she'd made when Luca put his arm around her waist to guide her towards the floor. The clasp was as light as thistledown, but even so it alerted every nerve-ending in her body.

Finally, Luca had the woman in his arms. Why it had been so important, he didn't know, but he'd seen her first in the theatre and had been fascinated by her total competence and composure, then, meeting her afterwards in the lounge, he'd felt attraction stir.

That, in itself, had been enough to confuse him. Lately he'd been so busy with his work, and plans for the new clinic, he'd had no time at all for a social life—a fact his long-term fiancée had pointed out with some bitterness, just before she'd flung the engagement ring at him and gone off to marry the industrialist who'd been after her for so long.

But that had been six months ago and half a world away. Now here he was, with another woman in his arms—a very different woman—one with something special about her—something that had drawn him to make a fool of himself with his compliments and behaviour earlier. Now he held her loosely, fearing she would break away if he tried to hold her close. Her tension was so palpable he could feel it vibrating between them.

But why?

She was beautiful. She must be used to men falling at her feet. She should carry the assurance that came with the combination of beauty and experience. Yet her tension suggested there was more behind her reaction to him than a wish for him to proceed more slowly.

He would find out.

'You like theatre work?'

Rachel nodded, and he suspected, as he watched her slide her tongue surreptitiously across her lips, that it had been safer to answer that way than to try to form words.

'You're good at it, I saw that. You chose it because it suits your skills?'

She didn't answer immediately, and he felt a hitch in the smooth movement of her feet, then she lifted her shoulders in a little shrug as if either his question or her reply was unimportant.

'It's detached,' she said, a slight smile curving up the left side of her lips. 'Working in Theatre, I don't need to get involved with either the patients or their families.'

A slight pause then her head tilted upward and warm golden brown eyes met his.

'I don't get involved with men either, Luca,' she said quietly.

And she meant it. He knew that immediately, but refused to be daunted.

'You've been hurt! I can see that in your—your defensiveness. Will you tell me what happened?'

He felt a tremor run through her body and regretted his curiosity, but that curiosity was part and parcel of who he was, and he could no more have not asked than he could have stopped his heartbeats.

'No!'

She whispered the word, almost under her breath, but he caught it anyway, and drew her just a fraction closer.

'That's all right,' he assured her. 'You don't know me, so why should you tell me personal things? My family all talk too much. We talk about everything— our hopes and dreams and fears and worries. We dramatise, cry, yell, fight, hold and hug each other over the talk we share, so I ask questions an American or Australian man might not ask.'

She looked up at him, a smile in the eyes that were widely spaced and slightly elongated, like the eyes of a very beautiful cat.

'And do you mind if you don't get answers?'

He couldn't help but respond to that smile.

'Ah, but I did get an answer. You don't get involved with men. You told me that much. So I remind you now I am not men in general.' He held her lightly so she wouldn't feel trapped. 'I am a man, singular, and we will be working together a lot of the time. If I promise to take it slowly, will you consider seeing something of me when we are both off duty?'

He heard the words and knew he'd said them, but in his head he was wondering why.

How much easier to find someone else to flirt with—the little secretary, Becky, for one? She would go out with him, show him the city that was her home and, he was reasonably certain, they would have a good time together.

But, glancing across to where Becky danced with Kurt, Luca knew it wouldn't work.

No, for some reason that defied rational argument, he knew if he was to enjoy a relationship with anyone during his short stay in Australia, it would have to be with the woman who danced so reluctantly in his arms.

Was it fate that Luca's temporary abode was in a high tower of serviced apartments right next to the very unserviced building—there wasn't even an elevator—where she and Kurt shared what their landlord called a two-bed flat? Kurt had made rude remarks—not to the landlord—about liking his beds flat, but they'd both known, after six months in Melbourne—learning the language, as Kurt said—that 'flat' down under didn't mean an even surface, but an apartment.

Not that the standard of accommodation had anything to do with Rachel's discomfort as she'd walked home from the party with the two men. Mostly it was due to Luca's presence, though anger had seethed as well because Kurt, in an excess of good spirits—no doubt brought on by an excess of the wine that had flowed—had asked the man to dinner the next evening.

Saturday night!

Which was fine, except her presence at the dinner table made it obvious she had no man in her life. Why else would she have been dateless on a Saturday night?

But Kurt had done the asking so she hoped she didn't appear desperate as well as dateless!

Kurt cooked a delicious meal, and was at his most charming best, but Rachel found the evening uncomfortable, and Luca's company unsettling. Physically unsettling in a way she couldn't remember ever feeling before.

Tension meant she had more than her usual two glasses of wine so when Luca asked, as he was taking his leave, if they would join him for dinner the following evening she thought it a wonderful idea and said, yes, her assent no sooner out than she heard Kurt pleading another engagement.

So here she was late on Sunday afternoon, surveying a wardrobe that consisted mostly of jeans and sweat pants with a variety of tops she wore according to the weather—short-sleeved if it was hot, long-sleeved if it was cold.

She did have one green T-shirt she particularly liked, but she'd worn it to death so it was faded and out of shape and she knew, if Kurt had been here, he'd have forbidden her to wear it.

So she'd wear the black one she'd picked up at a market in Melbourne and had never had occasion to wear, because it was definitely a 'going out' type top—V-necked, long-sleeved, slinky kind of fabric, with a feathery bird printed on it in some kind of gold paint.

Jeans would stop it looking too formal…

Why the hell was she doing this?

She didn't date—or if she did it was with men in whom she had not the slightest interest. Not that she was interested in Luca, not really. It was just some glitch in her body chemistry—some cellular attraction in her body to the pheromones he shed so effortlessly.

Working this out didn't make her feel any better.

Neither did Luca's behaviour, which was exemplary from the moment he collected her from her flat, walking her down the stairs with only an occasional touch on her elbow for support, holding an umbrella over her as he ushered her into the waiting taxi, talking casually about the weather, which had turned bleak and wet, and what he'd seen of Sydney through the rain when Alex and Annie had taken him for a drive earlier in the day.

The restaurant was above a row of shops and looked out over the promenade, the beach and further out to a turbulent dark ocean. White spray from the crashing waves lit its blackness, but it seemed to have a brooding power—not unlike the man with whom she shared a table.

'You like the ocean?' Luca, playing the perfect host.

'Love it! Though usually when I've been down here to Bondi I've seen it in happier moods.'

'I have raced on yachts across the Atlantic,' Luca said, 'but I prefer the Mediterranean where the weather is more predictable.'

'Of course,' Rachel said, again realising what worlds apart they were, that he could speak so casually of racing yachts and a sea she'd only heard and read of.

'You like boats?'

The question had been inevitable.

'The ones I've been on,' she said, then grinned at him. 'Ferries on Sydney Harbour! I live a long way from water back at home.'

'So tell me about your home.'

He was still being the good host, but 'home' wasn't a subject Rachel wanted to discuss. Once she was thinking of home, it would be too easy to think of other things. Fortunately, a waiter arrived, and began to list the specials available that night, and listening to his recital then discussing what they would eat diverted the conversation to food.

'You will have some wine?'

Rachel shook her head.

'Work day tomorrow, and a big work day. I know Alex has a TAPVR listed first up, and they can be tricky. And if the first op overruns its time, we'll be late all day, which is when people get frazzled.'

Luca smiled at her, and just about every cell in her body responded, so she had to remind them it was just a chemical reaction and nothing was going to happen, so to cool it.

They talked about the operation—far safer, especially as Rachel had assisted in so many total anomalous pulmonary venous return ops with Alex that she knew it inside out. And because talking work helped keep her mind off her physical problems, she asked Luca about his work—about the operations he liked doing—knowing most surgeons had their favourites.

'Transplants.' His answer was unequivocal. 'I haven't done many, but there is something about removing a terribly damaged heart and replacing it with a healthy one that fills me with wonder. I know the operation is only the first part of the battle, but I find that battle—to keep the patient stable, fight infection and rejection—a great challenge. It's a fight, so far, I've been fortunate enough to win, so perhaps that is why the operation is my favourite.'

The passion in his voice affected Rachel nearly as badly as the attraction. She understood it, because she loved her work in the same way. Every operation was a new challenge, and her total focus, whether she was handing instruments to the surgeon, suctioning, or massaging a tiny heart, was on providing the best possible outcome for the baby or child on the table in front of her.

She felt the bond between them but at the same time was aware this was a very different kind of attraction and an infinitely more worrying one.

Talking about work was still the best option so she asked about places he'd trained and surgeons with whom he'd studied.

It should have been safe, innocuous conversation, but beneath it the attraction still simmered, and when he passed her a bowl of freshly grated Parmesan cheese to sprinkle on her pasta and their fingers brushed together, she felt heat flash through her body.

Crikey, she was in trouble…

'Phil as a surgeon.'

And she was missing the conversation.

She looked at Luca—at the dark eyes, and bronzed skin, and strong-boned face—and tried desperately to guess what he'd been saying.

'He's terrific,' she managed to get out, hoping he'd asked her about Phil's ability.

He hadn't! That much was obvious from the delighted grin that spread across his face.

'You were thinking of other things?' he teased. 'Too much to hope it might have been of me.'

'Far too much!' she snapped—perhaps too snappishly! 'I was thinking about the TAPVR.'

'Ah!' Luca murmured, dark eyes smiling at her so she knew he didn't for a moment believe her. 'Of course!'

But those smiling dark eyes not only seemed to see right into her soul, they made her feel warm and excited and, damn it all, sexy!

And *that* feeling was so unfamiliar she had to mentally question it before deciding, yes, that's what it was.

Somehow she got through the rest of the meal, refusing dessert or coffee, anxious to get home now her hormones seemed to be totally out of control.

Again they took a cab, Luca paying the driver off outside Rachel's building before offering to walk her up the stairs.

She thought of the dim lighting on the landings and the temptation the gloom would provide and insisted she could walk up unattended.

'That is not right,' he protested. 'I should at least see you to the door.'

Rachel smiled at him.

'Not right but probably safer. I'm not at all sure about this situation, Luca. I meant it when I said I don't get involved with men.'

But her heart was thudding so loudly he could probably hear it, and her body was leaning towards his even before he put his hands on her shoulders and drew her close.

'It is up to you,' he said softly, the little puffs of air from the words brushing her cheek as he bent his head and kissed her on the lips.

By this time she was so wired—so jumpy—her brain forgot to tell her lips not to respond. And the heat she'd felt earlier with an accidental touch of fingers was nothing to what she now experienced.

Hard, hot and horrifyingly exciting—her lips clung to his as her body awoke from a long, long sleep and desire spiralled deeper and deeper into her body.

An impulse to drag him inside, rip off his clothes and give in to the urges she was feeling came from nowhere and her startled brain was actually considering it when two young lads walked by.

'Get a room!' one of them yelled.

Mortified by her thoughts *and* her behaviour, Rachel pushed away from the man who was causing havoc in her body, muttered her thanks for the meal and hurried into her building.

Luca watched her disappear—watched the door shut firmly behind her—and wondered just where things now stood between them.

He could no longer doubt that Rachel felt the attraction between them as strongly as he did.

So why was she resisting it?

Because they barely knew each other?

But giving in to it would help them know each other better...

He walked slowly along the pavement to his apartment building, thinking about attraction and a woman with red-gold hair and amber eyes who had, so unexpectedly, appeared in his life.

*   *   *

'I've called you all together because it's the first TAPVR operation we've done at Jimmie's and I wanted to run through the whole procedure.'

Alex stood on the dais at the front of the very small lecture room the unit used for staff meetings. Rachel, whose job today was to explain to the theatre staff exactly what they'd need, sat at a nearby table, uncomfortably aware of Luca in a seat directly behind her.

Not that she needed his presence to remind her of his…eruption—that was about the only word that fitted—into her life. He'd dominated her thoughts all weekend, both when she'd been with him, fighting the physical attraction, and when she hadn't been with him, when she'd wondered about it!

Now here she was, having to sit in front of the man and pretend nothing had happened—which it hadn't, apart from a mind-blowing, bone-melting, common-sense-numbing kiss.

Pretend nothing had happened, when her toes were curling every time she looked at him?

Could it be because of one kiss?

Was this what lust felt like?

And, if so, what did one do about it?

The problem was, she'd been out of circulation for too long for any of this to make sense. Remembered pain had been an effective barrier to involvement for the last four years, but she sensed the barrier was crumbling beneath the onslaught of her attraction to Luca.

But involvement led to vulnerability and she'd vowed never to be vulnerable again…

Never again!

Especially not when all that could possibly occur between herself and Luca was a brief affair.

She tried to focus on what Alex was saying. No doubt he'd begun by explaining that TAPVR stood for total anomalous pulmonary venous return. Put simply, Rachel knew, the blood vessels bringing oxygen-rich blood back from the lungs to the heart had hooked themselves up to the wrong place. Instead of coming into the left atrium to be pumped into the left ventricle and then out the aorta to be distributed throughout the body, some mistake had occurred during the heart's development and the blood returned to the right ventricle and was recirculated through the lungs, causing problems there while starving the rest of the body of oxygen.

'When does it happen?' someone asked, and Rachel realised she'd heard Alex's explanation so often before she was at the right place in her head.

'Usually during the first eight weeks of pregnancy, which is when the heart is developing from a double tube into a complex muscled organ.' Phil explained this to the nurse who'd asked the question and, looking at the young woman in the back row, Rachel realised the questioner was pregnant.

And worrying.

Been there, done that, have the T-shirt, Rachel thought, but, though she might act tough, remembered pain had her feeling sympathy for the pregnant woman.

Luca had also turned towards the speaker, and now he said, 'You shouldn't worry. You'll have had scans by now, and it would have shown up if your baby had a problem.'

It's nice he feels for people—even those he doesn't really know.

The thought sneaked up on Rachel and she had to

remind herself that Luca's niceness wasn't her concern.

The operation was her concern, and explaining what the theatre staff would be doing during it was her immediate concern.

Right now, apparently, because Alex was waving his hand in her direction and asking her to take over.

'You would make an excellent teacher,' Luca said an hour later when, the briefing over, he had managed to walk out of the room beside her. 'Have you thought of doing more academic work?'

'Not often,' Rachel told him honestly. 'I really love the theatre work I do, and Alex is good in that he encourages me to be part of the explanations as I was today, so I get to do a bit of teaching that way.'

Luca nodded.

'Yes, I like the way he includes everyone, theatre and PICU staff, in his briefings. I think I'll learn more than I even imagined I would from him—in administrative matters as well as surgical skills and techniques.'

Rachel felt a glow of pride for the man his team called Alexander the Great, then Luca was talking again.

'Have you worked with other surgeons back in the US? Are they all as meticulous in their planning? As thorough in their briefings?'

'I've occasionally assisted other surgeons. I suppose assisted sounds strange to you, but back at home I'm what's known as a PA—a physician's assistant. Anyway, since Alex joined the staff at the hospital where I trained, I've worked exclusively on his team, assisting whoever on the team is operating. Alex usually has a fellow working with him, Phil being the current one, and a registrar or surgeon in training, and then there are other surgeons, like yourself, on short-term visits.'

'So you would assist me if Alex asks me to be the lead surgeon in an operation while I am here?'

They'd talked as they walked towards the theatre the team used, Rachel fending off the strange sensations being close to Luca caused and answering his questions automatically. It was only after they'd parted, Luca to join Alex, who would have a final talk with the baby's parents, and she into the theatre to check all was ready, that she wondered if he'd been talking to her because he wanted to know more of the details of her job or to give him an excuse to walk with her.

Nice thought, that, but did she really want to break her commitment to non-involvement? Or want to have an affair with Luca just because her body was behaving badly?

The answer to both questions was no, but that was her brain talking at eight thirty-two in the morning, when the man was no longer in the vicinity so his body wasn't zapping hers with seductive messages.

Kurt was in the theatre, explaining the finer points of the heart-lung bypass machine to Ned, an Australian theatre sister who'd been seconded to their team and was being trained in the work Rachel did as a PA.

'Fantastic party Friday night,' Ned said cheerfully.

'Huh!' Rachel replied, but didn't elaborate. There was no need for the entire team to know she was in a tizz over Luca. She turned her attention to work, and addressed Ned and the other theatre staff.

'Although the echocardiograms suggest the pulmonary veins are connected to the right atrium instead of the left, the films are never as accurate as we'd like so we have to be prepared for surprises. I always make sure I've got extra patches and shunts in case they're needed, and the runner...' she nodded to the pregnant nurse '...knows where to put her hand on more if we need them.'

'I've got a full range ready,' the woman answered. 'I've put out the ones you usually use on the trolley, and have back-ups.'

She smiled at Rachel.

'I worked on an op with Phil a couple of weeks ago and he went through five shunts, snipping and shaving them, before he got one exactly the size he wanted. Since then I've made sure I've got plenty on hand.'

'Great,' Rachel said, and she meant it. The longer a baby was on bypass, the more chance there was of doing damage to its fragile circulatory system and organs. It was unacceptable to have hold-ups because the theatre personnel weren't properly prepared.

'The problem with TAPVR is that you can use so many patches and shunts. The surgeons have to detach the veins from wherever they are and patch the holes they left, then rejoin them up to the back of the left atrium and patch the hole between the two atria, which has usually been made bigger by the cardiologist during a catheterisation procedure. Then sometimes the veins are too small, and we either use a stent to hold them open or a patch to make them bigger, so, like the Scouts, we have to be prepared.'

She checked the trolley, automatically noting that

the instruments Alex would need were in the right places, then went to change.

'Teaching again,' a now familiar voice murmured.

Luca was standing in the doorway, and had obviously heard her little lecture to the nurses.

'That's not teaching,' she protested, while her body suggested her head had been wrong about the two decisions it had made earlier.

'Ah, but it is, and you are very effective.'

He touched her lightly on the shoulder, then went on his way, while she took her muddled thoughts into the changing room and wondered if physical attraction would get stronger or weaker if one gave in to it and enjoyed an affair purely for the satisfaction and undoubted delight it would bring.

CHAPTER THREE

THE operation took longer they any of them had expected, the baby's left atrium being small and underdeveloped, so in the end Alex had to splice the four pulmonary veins so he ended up with only two, then use another shunt to join them, attaching it to the tiny heart.

'It's a damn shame,' he said much later when he'd seen the baby's parents and had returned to where most of the team were gathered, holding a general debriefing. 'It means she'll need more operations as she grows, because the shunts won't grow with her.'

'I know you can use tissue from the baby to make patches,' Maggie said, her hands cupped around a mug of coffee. 'Could you also use a vessel from the baby instead of a shunt?'

'I've used veins taken from another part of the body for a small repair but for a vein as large as the pulmonary vein, I've never tried it,' Luca said, looking enquiringly at Alex.

'I have,' Alex said, 'and found it didn't work as effectively as the shunt. Because it was small, and possibly because it didn't like the insult of being transplanted from one site to another, it closed off almost immediately. Until we work out some way of successfully growing spare vessels inside the baby—which might not be that far away considering how science is advancing—then I believe we're better using shunts. At least the subsequent operations to replace them shouldn't require putting the patient on bypass.'

It was a fairly normal post-op conversation but there was nothing normal about Rachel's feelings, sitting as she was next to Luca who'd pulled a chair up close to her desk.

This distraction had to stop. So far she'd been able to keep one hundred per cent focussed in Theatre, all but forgetting Luca was in the room, but if, as he'd suggested, she was one day called upon to assist him, even a tiny distraction could lead to trouble.

She was due time off. She'd take it. Get right away. Maybe even, if she could get a cheap flight, go home to the States.

She was planning this little holiday in her head when she realised Alex was talking again. Something about a trip to Melbourne.

'I'm sorry, did you say you're going away? Does that mean we're all off duty for a few days?' She couldn't go home to the States for a few days but she could go north to somewhere warm—perhaps North Queensland.

Alex grinned at her.

'No, it doesn't mean you're all off duty for a few days. I know you're due time off, Rachel, but if you can just hang in for this week, I'm sure we can work something out after that.'

He paused and Rachel sensed something bad was coming—it was unlike Alex not to come right out with things.

'Problem is, Phil, Maggie, Kurt and I are flying to Melbourne tomorrow to do this op. We're taking an early morning flight, and will overnight there to make sure the baby's stable before we leave, then be back about ten on Wednesday.'

'Not me?'

She didn't particularly want to go to Melbourne, but if the core of the team was going, why not her?

Alex smiled again.

'It's not that I wouldn't like to take you—but you know you trained that theatre sister down there well enough to do your job. Besides, I need you to be here.'

Another hesitation, so Rachel prompted him.

'You need me to be here?'

A nod this time—no smile.

'I do indeed. We've an op scheduled for midday on the day we get back—a first-stage op for a baby born with HLHS—hypoplastic left heart syndrome. The Flying Marvels, that organisation of private plane owners who volunteer their time and planes, are flying the baby and his parents to Sydney early tomorrow morning. I need someone to do the briefing. Luca can explain the operation to them—what we'll be doing—but I'd like you, Rach...' his eyes met hers in silent apology '...to explain the post-op situation to them. What to expect when the baby comes out of Theatre—the tubes and drains and special equipment that will be protruding from his body.'

The words hit against her skin like sharp stones, but with the entire team looking at her with varying degrees of interest or concern, depending on how long they'd known her, she could hardly throw a tantrum and refuse Alex's request. Especially as he wouldn't have asked if there'd been any alternative! She'd be here, she knew his work, she knew exactly what the baby would be attached to when he left Theatre—so who better to explain?

'No worries,' she said, using a phrase she'd heard repeatedly during her time in Australia. And if her voice was hoarse and the words sounded less convincing than when an Aussie said them, that was too bad. It was the best she could do under the circumstances.

With duties handed out, the meeting broke up, though Alex signalled for Luca and Rachel to stay.

'Luca, if you wouldn't mind having dinner with Annie and me tonight, I'll give you a run-through of how we do the procedure. Actually, Rachel, you should come too if you can. I'll give Annie a quick call to let her know she has extra mouths to feed, then, Rachel, can I see you privately for a moment?'

Rachel nodded glumly, and watched him walk behind the partition that provided the only bit of privacy in the big room.

Luca turned to her.

'Did I imagine something going on there, a tension in the air? Is Alex perhaps aware you don't like to get involved with patients? If so, why is he asking you to do this?'

Luca's dark eyes scanned her face and the sympathetic anxiety in them, and in his voice, weakened the small resolve Rachel had built up during a kissless day.

'He's asked because there's no one else, and he wants to see me privately to give me a hug and say he's sorry he had to ask.'

'You know him so well?'

Rachel smiled at Luca's incredulity.

'On Alex's team we're a bit like family—a grown-up family that doesn't live in each other's pockets—but we've shared good times and bad times and we stick together through them all.'

Alex appeared as she finished this explanation and Luca politely left the room, though the scene panned out exactly as Rachel had foretold.

'I'm sorry to ask you to do this,' Alex said, giving her a big, warm hug.

'That's OK,' Rachel told him, and though, deep in her heart she wasn't at all sure it *was* OK, she was also beginning to think it was time!

'You'll be all right with it?'

She stepped back and looked at the man with whom she'd worked for a long time.

'And if I'm not?' she teased, then was sorry when she saw him frown.

'Of course I'll be all right,' she hurried to assure him. 'Quit worrying.'

He hugged her once again, but she doubted he'd obey her last command. Alex worried over the well-being of all his team.

She'd just have to prove herself tomorrow.

Or maybe she shouldn't, because she certainly didn't want this patient-contact stuff to become a habit...

Luca was waiting for them outside, and, though she could practically hear the questions he wanted to ask hammering away in his head, he said nothing, simply falling in beside her as they walked to the elevator, and staying close in a protective way that should have aggravated Rachel, but didn't.

He held her jacket for her before they walked out into the cool spring air, and brushed his fingers against her neck. His touch sent desire spiralling through her, although she knew it was a touch of comfort not seduction.

This was madness. It was unbelievable that physical attraction could be so strong. And as surely as it fired her body, it numbed her mind so she had difficulty thinking clearly—or thinking at all a lot of the time!

So she didn't. She walked between the two men, and let their conversation wash across her, enjoying the sharp bite of the southerly wind and the smell of smoke from wood fires in the air.

Annie greeted them as if she hadn't seen them an hour or so earlier, and introduced Luca to her father, Rod, and Henry, her dog.

Henry, Rachel noticed, seem to approve of Luca, bumping his big head against Luca's knee and looking up for more pats.

There's no scientific proof that dogs are good judges of character, she told herself, but that didn't stop her feeling pleased by Henry's behaviour.

Which brought back thoughts of brain transplants...

Annie ordered them all to the table, already set with cutlery, plates and thick slices of crunchy bread piled high in a wicker basket in the middle. She then brought out a pot only slightly smaller than a cauldron, and set it on the table.

'Lamb shanks braised with onions and cranberries,' she announced. 'Help yourselves, and take plenty of bread to mop up the juice.'

Discussion was forgotten as they tucked into the appetising meal, and it was only when they were all on second helpings that Alex began to explain exactly what the upcoming operation entailed.

'It is the same procedure I use,' Luca told him, when Alex had finished speaking. 'I'm confident I can explain it well to the parents. I've seen you in action with explanations, remember, and I know you always tell the families of the problems that can arise during an operation, as well as the hoped-for outcomes.'

Alex nodded.

'We talk about "informed decisions",' he said, 'but I fail to see how parents can make informed decisions if they aren't aware their child could die, or suffer brain or liver damage, during open-heart surgery. And it is equally important they know they will still have a very sick child after surgery, and be prepared to care for that child for however long it takes.'

'In your experience, do most parents accept this?' Luca asked. 'Have you had parents who opted not to let you operate?'

Alex hesitated, his gaze flicking towards Rachel.

'Many of them over the years,' he admitted. 'And I have to respect their decision, though in some cases I was sure the outcome would have been good. But family circumstances come into play as well. Not all families can afford a child who will need a series of operations and constant medical attention for the rest of his life, yet this is all we can offer them in some cases.'

'It is a terrible choice, isn't it?' Luca said.

'It is, but I refuse to end a pleasant evening on such a gloomy note,' Annie declared. 'Dad, tell us some murder stories—that's far more fun.'

Rod, an ex-policeman who now wrote mysteries, obliged with some tales of bizarre and intriguing true-life cases from long ago.

* * *

'Rod's stories might not have been ideal dinner party conversation,' Luca said, as Rachel guided him on a short cut home across a well-lit park, 'but they got us away from that depressing conversation.'

He spoke lightly, but he'd been sitting beside Rachel at the dinner table and had felt her tension—which had begun back when Alex had asked her to speak to the patient's parents—escalating during the meal. There was a story behind it and much as he wanted to know more, he was reluctant to ask, fearing it might break the fragile bond he believed was developing between them.

He glanced towards her. She was walking swiftly, her hands thrust deep in her jacket pockets, her head bent as if she had to concentrate on the path beneath her feet, but the unhappiness she was carrying was so strong it was like a dark aura around her body.

This was not the Rachel he knew, she of the glorious hair, and the sunny smile, and the smart remark. This was a person in torment, and her pain, unexpectedly, was reaching out and touching him. He could no more ignore it than he could refuse to help a child in trouble.

He put his arm around her and guided her to a seat in the shadow of a spreading tree. Her lack of resistance reassured him, and once they were seated he tucked her body close to his and smoothed his hand across her hair, holding her for a moment in the only way he knew to offer comfort.

'Will you tell me what it is that hurts you so much? Why Alex had to give you a hug?'

She turned and looked at him, studying his face as if he were a stranger, then she looked away, back down at the ground, her body so tight with tension he was sure he could hear it crackling in the air around them.

Then she nodded, and he held his breath, wondering if she'd tell the truth or make up some story to stop him asking more.

But when it came he knew it was not make-believe, because every word was riven with raw pain.

'Years ago, I was going out with this man. I found I was pregnant, we got married, the pregnancy was normal, the scans showed nothing, but the baby was early. I was staying with my parents at the time and had the baby in the local town hospital. He was diagnosed with HLHS, which was ironic considering I was working even then with Alex. Yet I hadn't given having a baby with a congenital heart defect more than a passing thought. I haemorrhaged badly during the birth, and had blood dripping into me, and drugs numbing my mind, so the paediatrician spoke to my husband, explained the situation, told him to talk to me and think about the options, which included transferring the baby to Alex's hospital. But that didn't happen. My husband made the decision not to operate.'

Rachel's voice had grown so faint Luca barely heard the final words, and he was repeating them to himself—and feeling something of the horror and loss Rachel must have experienced—when she spoke again.

'It didn't matter, as it turned out,' she said harshly. 'The baby died that night, before he could have been transferred.'

Dio! Luca thought, drawing the still-grieving woman closer to his side and pressing kisses of comfort, not desire, on the shining hair.

'Oh, Rachel, what can I say?' he said, and knew the emotion he was feeling had caused the gruffness in his voice. 'You are a very special person. I knew this from your work, but to know your sorrow and see you helping other people's babies, assisting them to live—that shows more courage than I would have. More than most people in the entire world would have.'

He felt the movement of her shoulders and knew she was shaking off his praise, and perhaps a little of her melancholy. Something she confirmed when she straightened up, moving away from him, and said, 'It was four years ago. I don't usually crack up like this. I guess Alex asking me to talk to the parents brought back memories I thought I'd put away for ever.'

'No matter how deeply you might bury it in your brain, I doubt you could ever put the loss of a child completely away,' Luca told her, hearing in his voice the echoes of his own buried memories.

She stood up and looked down at him, and even in the shadows he could see the sadness in the slow smile she offered him.

'Maybe not,' she said, 'but you do get past thinking of it every minute of every day, so maybe now it's time for me to get past seeing other babies who are ill, and thinking of my Reece.'

Luca stood up too, and took her hand, the clasp of a friend.

What happened to your husband? he wanted to ask. Her name was her own, he knew that, and she wore no ring. Had she divorced the man who'd made the decision not to try to save her baby? Because of that decision?

But surely, with his wife so ill as well, it could not

be held against him, especially as the baby died anyway!

'My husband visited me in hospital the next day,' she said suddenly, making Luca wonder if he'd asked his question out loud. 'He brought his girlfriend and explained that she, too, was pregnant, and he'd like a quickie divorce so he could marry her.'

She stopped again, and this time, in the light shed by a lamp beside the path, he saw mischief in the sadness of her smile.

'I threw a bedpan at him. Best of all, I'd just used it. The pan hit him on the nose—I'd always been good at softball—but she didn't escape the fallout. Petty revenge, I know, but it sure made me feel better.'

Luca put his arms around her and hugged her tight.

'Remind me never to upset you when you have a scalpel in your hand,' he teased.

Then they continued on their way, friends, he felt, not would-be lovers.

Not tonight!

CHAPTER FOUR

IT WAS both better and worse than Rachel had thought it would be, walking into the room where two anxious parents sat beside their infant son. Better, she had to admit, because Luca was there, not holding her hand but standing shoulder to shoulder with her, as if he knew she needed some physical support.

Worse, because the baby was so beautiful. She tried so hard not to look at whole babies, preferring to concentrate on the little bit of them left visible by the shrouding green drapes of the theatre.

But this baby drew her eyes and she looked at him while Luca introduced them both.

She shook hands automatically, her attention still on the physical perfection of the tiny child. Smooth soft skin, downy fair hair, rosebud mouth and dusky eyelashes lying against his cheeks. A chubby baby so outwardly perfect her arms ached to hold him and hug him to her body.

The perfection, however, was spoilt by the tube in his nose, and the hum of the ventilator, and the drip taped to his fat little starfish hand.

'He's wonderfully healthy,' Luca said, examining the baby boy.

'Apart from his heart,' the father said.

'Yes, but some babies with the same problem have not done well *in utero*,' Luca told them, 'so they are very fragile even before we operate. Your…' He hesitated momentarily and Rachel filled in for him.

'Bobbie.'

Luca smiled at her, a special smile that started the faintest whisper of attraction happening again.

Damn, she'd thought she'd got rid of that last night!

'Your Bobbie,' Luca was saying, 'is so well, we will not hesitate to operate unless you decide otherwise.'

He went on to explain exactly what the team would do, how long it would take, and what would lie ahead for the family.

'You will have been told,' he said, 'that with hypoplastic left heart syndrome, this will be the first of three operations to rebuild Bobbie's heart into a properly functioning mechanism. This first, which we call the Norwood, is the most complex, and carries the most risk, and Bobbie will have the longest recovery time from it. Maybe three or four weeks in hospital. Then, when he's four to six months old, we do the second stage, a Glenn, and finally when he is two or three, we will do an operation called a Fontan. These operations are usually called after the surgeon who first performed them, which is why they have strange names.'

'And then? After three operations?' the mother asked.

'He will still need constant monitoring and regular visits to the cardiologist, but the outlook is quite good,' Rachel said, knowing it because she'd read up on all the outcomes for the operations they did—and practically knew the stuff on HLHS by heart. 'He won't have any significant developmental delays—apart from those caused by frequent hospitalisation during his first few years. He'll be able to play sport, though he shouldn't undertake really vigorous exercise.'

'So these operations won't make him totally better? They won't make him normal?'

It was the mother again, and Rachel, though she doubted anyone could define 'normal' satisfactorily, understood her concern.

'No. We can remake his heart so it works, but it will never be a so-called normal heart,' she said, then she glanced at Luca.

He must have read her thoughts for he nodded.

She turned back to the worried parents.

'Look, you two have a lot to think about. Why don't you talk about it? And when you want more answers, or want to know more about the operation or Bobbie's post-op state, ask the sister to page us and we'll come straight back. We'll just be in our office on the other side of the PICU.'

Bobbie's parents looked relieved, so Rachel ushered Luca through the door.

'We tell them too much at once,' she said to him, upset and frustrated because she could sense the parents' doubts. 'I know we have to explain it all to them, because otherwise they can't make an informed decision, but it's hard for people to assimilate all the medical terms and the possible outcomes when they're worried sick about their baby to begin with.'

Luca nodded. 'I sometimes think it is the worst part of my job—that, and telling parents I could not save their baby.'

His choice of words startled Rachel.

'Do you say "I" or "we"?' she demanded, only realising how strident she must have sounded when Luca turned to her in surprise.

'I say "I",' he responded.

'But that's taking all the responsibility on yourself, and that puts more pressure on your shoulders. It's a team effort. You should say "we".'

Luca smiled at her.

'I'm serious,' Rachel told him, 'You're operating on tiny human beings. There's enormous pressure on you anyway, so why add more?'

He touched her lightly on the shoulder.

'I am not smiling because I think you are wrong, but because of your passion. It tells me much about you.'

His words slid like silk across her skin and she shivered in the warm hospital air. Last night she'd thought friendship was replacing the attraction she'd felt for Luca, yet one word, huskily spoken in his beguiling accent, and her nerve-endings were again atwitter while her body hungered for his touch.

Passion!

She wasn't entirely sure she understood exactly what it was. But unless she found something else to put the brakes on what was happening, she might soon be finding out.

Back at her desk, Rachel took a cautious sip of coffee, sure it would be too hot, then glanced at Luca as he fished in his pocket.

'I had my pager set to vibrate rather than buzz. It seems the parents have talked and we're needed again. Only this time it will be your turn.'

He looked anxiously at her, banishing her thoughts of passion, which, contrarily, made Rachel angry.

'I didn't tell you stuff last night to make you feel

sorry for me, but because I thought you should know. I'm a professional—I'll do my job in there.'

'I know you will,' he said, 'but do not tell me what to feel in my heart.'

He walked away, leaving her to follow, uncertainty dogging her footsteps, though this time it was to do with Luca, not with what lay immediately ahead.

Do not tell him what to feel in his heart?

He barely knew her, yet he was saying things that confused *her* heart.

Forget it!

Non-involvement, that's your go!

Think work!

She caught up with him so they walked into Bobbie's room together. Luca answered all the questions the parents had, then talked again about the procedure, before explaining that Rachel would tell them about the immediate post-operative period.

Rachel looked at the couple, wondering how much they could absorb, then looked again at the baby on the bed.

So beautiful her heart ached for him, knowing what lay ahead.

'He's already on the ventilator, so you probably understand that what it does is breathe for him—not all the time, but when and as he needs extra help. It saves him the energy he would use if he was breathing entirely on his own.'

'So he'll be on that again when he comes out?' the woman asked, and Rachel nodded.

'I was reading in the papers someone gave us where it's sometimes hard to wean a baby off a ventilator,' the father put in. 'Is that likely to happen?'

'It can happen,' Rachel said cautiously, then she

smiled. 'But we rarely send our kids off to their first day of school with a bottle of oxygen so you'd better believe we can get them off!'

Both parents smiled back at her and Rachel knew the tense atmosphere in the room had relaxed slightly.

Time to take advantage of it.

'He'll have a nasogastric tube—up his nose and down into his stomach—to keep his stomach clear of acid and gas that might have built up during the op. He can also be fed nutrients using this tube. Will you be expressing breast milk for him?'

The woman nodded.

'Good, because not having to change from formula to breast milk will be better for him later when he's able to feed for himself. If necessary, the hospital dietician might advise staff to give him supplemental calories, which will be added to the milk. These will help him grow while allowing him to take in less fluid. Speaking of which, he'll have a urinary catheter, and he will be given diuretics to make sure his body isn't retaining excess water. What happens is the surgery upsets all the body—especially in a body this small—so during the immediate post-op period other organs might not do their jobs as well as they should.'

She paused, knowing all the information must be mind-boggling to the parents, and wanting to give them time to assimilate at least a little of it. Then, thinking carefully so every word would count, she continued.

'Sometimes we leave a tube in the abdomen to help the liver flush out toxins and he'll definitely be on a heart monitor and maybe have a tiny pacemaker to keep his heartbeats regular while he recovers from the insult of the operation. It will look like a thin wire protruding from his body, and will be attached to a battery-operated device that will stimulate the heart if it falters.'

'So he'll come out with tubes and drains and wires poking out of him, and his chest all sewn up, and we have to stay calm?'

The baby's father had stood up and was by the bed as he spoke, smoothing his long forefinger across his son's head, looking, Rachel guessed, at the perfection of a body that would soon be marred.

'No, you don't have to stay calm,' Rachel told him. 'You can be as upset as you like. You should be. The little fellow is going to go through major surgery that would take an adult months to recover from, but your little boy will probably be out of here—the cardiac paediatric intensive care unit—in two or three days, a week at the most. Infants are amazingly resilient. Once he leaves here he'll have another couple of weeks in the babies' ward, then you can take him home.'

'You will be given plenty of instructions and in-formation and support when you take him home,' Luca said, sitting in the husband's chair beside the woman and taking her hand. He must have noticed how distressed she was getting, Rachel realised, while she herself had been yammering on and probably making things worse, not better.

'I'm sorry,' she said, coming to kneel beside the distressed mother. 'It's hard to take in but it's best that you know what's going to happen.'

'It's not that, it's the decision,' the woman cried. 'Why do we have to decide? Why can't the doctors decide?'

'You have to decide because he is your baby,' Luca said gently.

'Then tell me what to do for him—tell me what is best,' the woman demanded. 'What would you do if it was your baby?'

The air in the warm room grew very cold—or at least the bit of it surrounding Rachel's body developed an icy chill. She looked at the baby on the bed—twice the size her Reece had been—outwardly perfect, apart from a blue tinge to his lips. Jake had known he would be leaving her—that decision had been made—so had he listened to the doctors explaining what they had to do, then decided Rachel wouldn't be able to cope with a very sick baby on her own?

Was that why he'd decided to say no to an operation?

'Is your marriage strong?' she asked, and realised she must have spoken harshly because all three adults in the room spun to look at her. 'That's probably a rude question, but it's important, because you'll need each other's strength to get you through this. There'll be bad times, and worse times, and you'll need each other more than you ever realised. So it has to be a united decision. You must both agree to it, and not hold grudges or lay blame later on. But, that said, then, yes. I'm not a doctor, but if Bobbie were my baby, I'd opt for the operation. I'd give him a chance, and if it doesn't work—if the worst happens—at least you'll know you tried.'

Realising she'd become too emotionally involved with the entire situation, she tried a casual shrug and smiled at the bemused parents.

'But, then, as I said, I'm not a doctor,' she said. 'It's Luca you should be asking.'

She hurried out of the room, sure if she stayed another moment she'd burst into tears.

Crikey! What was this about? She hadn't cried in years! It couldn't have been seeing the baby, could it?

Or was it because she'd broken her vow not to get involved?

She blinked and sniffed back tears, fumbling in her pocket for a handkerchief, glad she'd made for the less-used service foyer and no one was around to see or hear her unprofessional behaviour.

'Are you all right? *Dio*, it was wrong of Alex to ask you to do that.'

Luca was there, his arm around her, drawing her close. And for a moment she gave in to the need to be held and comforted, then she pushed away, knowing he was comforting her for all the wrong reasons.

'No, it wasn't wrong,' she said, smiling weakly at the man who looked so concerned for her. 'Alex probably knew me better than I knew myself. I had to get past what happened—I should have got past it long ago—and as long as I was avoiding situations like that, I wasn't going to.'

She turned away, and leant against the wall—not as comforting as Luca's body but infinitely safer.

'I didn't get upset over losing Reece—not when I was talking to the parents. I got upset because for the first time I looked at Jake's—my husband's—decision from his point of view. He'd been unfaithful, sure, but we hadn't been that committed to each other when we married. We'd been going out together, having fun, and vaguely thinking our relationship might lead somewhere. When I realised I was pregnant, he thought I should have an abortion but, as a nurse, the idea of doing such a thing horrified me, so we made the absolutely wrong decision right there and then, and got married. Don't get me wrong, I loved Jake but I knew he didn't love me in the same way. By the time Reece arrived, although I dearly wanted that baby—already loved him, if you know what I mean—we both knew the marriage wasn't working.'

An aide walked past and looked curiously at them.

'This is not a conversation I should be having here,' Rachel said, straightening off the wall. 'Or with you,' she added, as embarrassment at how frank she'd been began to surface.

'It is often easier to talk to strangers, though I hope I am more than that to you,' Luca said. 'And here and now is as good a place and time as any. Will you finish telling me?'

Rachel thought about it, then decided she might feel a whole lot better if she did finish, if she explained to someone—anyone—the revelation she'd had in that room.

'I've always blamed Jake. I thought the decision not to operate stemmed from selfishness, from him not wanting to be saddled with a sick child for the foreseeable future, but in there, talking to those parents, I realised he'd already made his big decision. He was moving on, child or no child, and he was thinking of me, and how I'd cope. I'd have had to give up work, and he knew how much I loved my job and how much it meant to me.'

She looked bleakly at Luca.

'I've blamed him all these years for that decision yet I realise now he made it for my sake.'

Luca thought he knew a fair bit about women. After all, he'd grown up with four sisters. But this woman's pain was new to him—new because he couldn't grasp where it was coming from.

But his lack of understanding didn't make her condition any less real. He took her in his arms and though she stiffened momentarily she then relaxed enough to return the embrace, holding him close against her for a moment, then lifting her head to look into his eyes.

'Thank you for listening,' she said softly. 'For being there.'

Amber eyes repeated the message, and her lips parted softly, so it seemed only natural to kiss her.

Very gently! Feeling her emotional fragility, and not wanting to take advantage of it.

Not wanting to take advantage?

Weird thought, that, when the idea foremost in his mind most of the time was getting her into his bed!

Equally gently, he disengaged.

'Come,' he said. 'The parents are talking again with other family members, and a man I think is a priest has also come to talk to them. We didn't have time to drink our coffee last time. Let's go to the rooms and try again. The parents know to page us if they need us.'

He wanted to put his arm around her shoulders again, but knew from the way she held herself that it would be wrong. She was gathering her strength, renewing her reserves of courage—he could see it in the proud tilt of her head, and the stiffening of her spine—and he guessed she would not welcome sympathy right now.

'Shoot, but I'd hate to be Alex—or you, for that

matter—doing this stuff before every single operation.'

She was striding towards their suite, and threw the remark over her shoulder at him, confirming his reading of her change in attitude.

'Not all of our conversations with parents concern life-or-death decisions,' he reminded her.

'No, I guess not,' she said soberly, then she turned and smiled at him. 'You were right—talking to a stranger definitely helped. Kurt's been telling me for years I should see an analyst. Maybe that's how psychologists and psychiatrists achieve their success—simply by being strangers mixed-up people can talk to.'

Luca would have liked to protest the stranger tag, but he sensed there was a brittle quality to Rachel's change of mood so he said nothing, merely offering to fix the coffee. When Becky, who was at her desk, said she'd do it, Luca took himself across to the desk he used and made notes about the talk they'd had with the little patient's parents.

He would then have to check on the baby they'd operated on yesterday, while no doubt Rachel would be busy preparing the theatre for the operation.

'Coffee for the sexy Italian!' Becky said, depositing a mug of strong black coffee on his desk, then put a small tray with two chocolate-coated biscuits beside it. 'And sweets for the sweet,' she added cheekily, pointing at the biscuits.

Luca had to smile. She flirted as naturally as she breathed, the pretty blonde Becky. What puzzled him was his lack of inclination to flirt back. Certainly his pursuit of Rachel wasn't getting far, and now that he understood her reluctance to get involved he doubted it would progress at all.

Yet something apart from her glorious hair attracted him, and beyond that he was coming more and more to think what an asset she'd be at his clinic. If he stole her heart, could he steal her away from Alex?

Not an honourable thought at all, but beneath their emotional exteriors most Italians were innately practical.

He nodded to himself, pleased to have this sorted out in his mind, though he doubted Americans could think as practically when love came into it. In his experience, love to them came with roses and chocolates and heart-shaped balloons—practicality was nowhere to be found.

He wrote his notes and drank his coffee, then began to worry why he hadn't been paged. Alex would be back soon and would want to know if the operation was to go ahead. In fact, Alex fully expected it would go ahead, having already spoken to the parents via a phone conference hook-up at the hospital where the baby had been born.

So if he, Luca, with Rachel, had ruined this plan with their explanations, how would Alex react?

'I think we should see if they've reached a decision before Alex gets back.'

As if summoned by his thoughts, Rachel stood at his desk. Luca nodded his agreement, and pushed his chair back, straightening up while Rachel waited.

'You don't have to come,' he told her, not wanting to subject her to more distress.

'They might have questions about post-op care,' she replied, in a voice that told him not to argue. So, together, yet in separate worlds, they walked towards the baby's room, where the man in the clerical collar was the only person waiting for them.

'The Archers have asked me to speak to you on their behalf,' he said. 'They have decided not to go ahead with the operation on baby Bobbie.'

Luca heard Rachel's gasp and moved closer to her. They might be inhabiting different worlds, but her world right now needed support.

'But he's so healthy,' she protested, and Luca took her hand, squeezing it to show his sympathy but also to warn her to think before she spoke.

'It is the parents' decision,' he reminded her, then he turned to the priest. 'Can you tell them we understand, but that Dr Attwood, who is head of the team, will need to hear it from them when he gets in from his trip to Melbourne.'

The man nodded. 'I'll tell them. It'll be hard for them, but I'll be with them.'

He looked from Luca to Rachel, then back to Luca before he spoke again.

'They didn't reach this decision easily, and they are deeply upset about having to make it. But they have other children—four—and in giving so much to this one, with regular trips to the city for his check-ups with specialists after the three operations, they would be denying the others. That is part of it. The other part is the uncertainty of the outcome. Even with the operations there are no guarantees that Bobbie will be healthy. Today it is hard for them to say they will let him go, but to lose him when they have loved and nurtured him for maybe four or five years—how much harder would that be? These are their thoughts.'

Luca felt the cold tenseness of Rachel's fingers and squeezed them, silently begging her not to argue—

not to fight for this baby's one chance at life. They had given the parents all the facts they needed to make a decision—to not respect that decision now would be deplorable.

The priest offered his hand to Luca, hesitated in front of Rachel, then made do with a farewell nod and left the room. Rachel sank into a chair, and though Luca guessed her legs would no longer hold her up he still urged her to her feet.

'Come. The parents will want to sit with Bobbie, and there are alternative arrangements that must be made,' he said. 'We'll find somewhere else.'

He guided her out of the room and, because it was closest, chose the little bedroom just off the PICU used by on-duty doctors at night.

'Here, sit!' he said, gently easing her onto the bed. Then he squatted in front of her and took her cold hands in his.

'Alex will talk to them. Maybe that will change their minds,' he said, hoping to wipe the dazed, blank look from her eyes.

She shook her head so violently her hair flew out in a wide arc the colour of molten gold.

'No, you were right. We told them what they needed to know, and they put that information with the other circumstances of their lives and decided. I have no doubt it is the right decision for them, but that baby, Luca?'

Desperate gold-amber eyes met his.

'He is so beautiful. To just let him die! It seems so unfair. So many people have healthy babies they don't really want or need, yet that one…'

She began to cry, not noisily but with deep, gulping sobs, then shook her head as if to shake the misery away and straightened once again. He wondered if she practised yoga, for she breathed deeply now, and he could see the inner strength he had seen before shoring up her defences. She even found a smile of sorts, though it was so pathetic it made Luca's chest hurt.

'Alex *will* be pleased! Not! He spoke as if the op was definitely on. The team members were coming back from Melbourne expressly to do it.' She glanced at her watch. 'Is there time to let them know it's off? They might prefer to stay on down there.'

She looked at Luca, who'd shifted to a chair, and continued, 'My brain's not working properly. Of course there's no time. It's a short flight—they must be almost back in Sydney by now.' A pause, then she added, 'I'm so sorry I fell apart all over you. This isn't the normal me, you know. I'm Rachel-who-can-cope-with-anything!'

Her courage was like a hand gripping and squeezing at Luca's heart, but he found a smile to give back to her.

'I think it is normal to feel emotional about a situation such as this. If we, as medical people, divorced ourselves from all our emotional reactions, we would become automatons instead of human beings. Medicine is about humanity, and we should all remember it—and be grateful, not negative, when we are reminded of it.'

'Spoken like a true Italian,' Rachel teased, and Luca knew she was feeling better, although her words reminded him of the thoughts he'd had earlier—emotion versus practicality!

'Contrary to what the world at large might think,

we are not entirely ruled by our emotions,' he told her.

'No?' She was still teasing, but this time she sounded more relaxed and he knew she was recovering. He was considering his reply—he would tell her about the practical side of the Italian psyche— when she spoke again.

'So if I kissed you here and now, just a thank-you-for-being-there-for-me kind of kiss, would you respond, or tell me to get back to work?'

His heart upped its beat, and his body tightened, but the kiss she brushed across his lips was definitely a thank-you-for-being-there-for-me kind of kiss.

He could, of course, take hold of her shoulders and draw her close to respond but, though Rachel might read it as a think-nothing-of-it kiss, his body might be misled into thinking it was serious, and walking around the hospital with an obvious erection wasn't something he could contemplate.

'You are tempting fate, my beautiful Rachel,' he said softly, then he stood up, touched her lightly on the head, and left the room.

CHAPTER FIVE

RACHEL followed, but more slowly, knowing she would have to walk past the baby's room, and not sure how her muddled emotions would react.

If she hadn't been so stubborn about not getting involved with their tiny patients, would she have recovered from Reece's death more swiftly?

Would she feel less bad now about the decision Bobbie's parents had taken?

Had she been holding back her recovery through cowardice?

And if non-contact with babies had been crippling her, then what was her non-involvement with men doing?

'You're only thinking that because you're attracted to Luca,' she muttered to herself as she made her way back to the rooms. 'Involvement with men is entirely different to involvement with babies. Involvement with men leads to pain.'

You are such a wimp!

Fortunately she'd stopped thinking aloud and this last admonition was in her head, so Becky, who'd looked up as Rachel walked through the door, didn't hear it.

'The boss is back. He phoned from the airport. ETA at the hospital in twenty minutes.'

'Great!' Rachel found she was muttering again. Where was Luca? If he didn't turn up, would she have to tell Alex of the decision?

Determined not to think any more about the baby, or the past, or even Luca, she went to her desk and grabbed all the untended mail sitting in her in-tray. It had been weeks since she'd seen the bottom of it, dealing with urgent matters and shuffling the rest back into the tray for some day when she had plenty of time.

Like today, because there was no op this afternoon...

She turned the pile over and started at the bottom, staring at an invitation to attend a theatre nurses' seminar two weeks ago.

Binned it and lifted the next item. A circular advertising a range of clothing for theatre nurses. Why on earth had she kept that? The hospital supplied their scrubs and who cared what they wore beneath them?

She flipped the paper over, saw a phone number printed on the back and smiled.

Scott Douglas, the registrar who was working with the team, had written down his home phone number. It had been after he'd asked her out for the fifth or possibly the sixth time, and he'd finally said, 'OK, when you feel like company, you call me!'

Right now a night out with Scott might be what she needed. She could ease back into male-female involvement without the high risk attached to doing it with Luca.

But Scott had had a pretty brunette with him at Maggie and Phil's party, and they'd seemed to be quite attached to each other.

She binned the leaflet with the number on it. Too late to use it now!

Her theatre nurses' association magazine, forwarded on from her US address, came next, and she shoved it in her handbag. She'd read it at home to-night.

An invitation to her cousin's wedding. She'd already sent a gift, so why had she kept the invite?

She turned it over, wondering if it too might have another pencilled message, but apart from two golden, entwined hearts, the other side was bare.

'Ah, golden hearts—you are a little sentimental after all?'

Luca's voice startled her so much she glowered at him, though her pulse had accelerated at the sound of his voice—badly enough for her to consider pulling the circular out of the bin and phoning Scott tonight, brunette or no brunette.

'This is how sentimental I am,' she said, and dropped the invitation into the bin.

Luca nodded, as if acknowledging her rebuttal, then settled into the other chair at the desk and said, 'Alex is back. He is talking to the Archers.'

Seconds later, Kurt joined them, propping himself against the desk and lifting one eyebrow as he looked her way.

'Good trip?' she asked, hoping her reaction to Luca's closeness wasn't noticeable to her friend.

'Successful,' he said, but he sounded tired.

Rachel raised her eyebrows, and Kurt hesitated, then said, 'I don't know, Rach. We do such terrible things to those fragile babies, then expect them to get over it. What about the ones who don't? Or the ones who suffer brain damage while on pump? Or have a stroke later because an air bubble has escaped someone's attention and filtered through their bloodstream to the brain?'

'Statistically, that rarely happens in Alex's ops,'

Rachel reminded him, wondering if he'd already heard this afternoon's operation wasn't going ahead.

'I know, but there was a little boy in the PICU down there in Melbourne. Surgeons had fixed his heart, but he'd had a stroke two days after the op. The parents were blaming the surgery, and they were probably right. It just makes me wonder about where and when to draw a line, that's all.'

He stood up again, and moved restlessly around the desk, then shook off his negative mood and smiled at Luca.

'Well,' he demanded, 'did you take advantage of my absence to get this woman into bed?'

'Kurt!'

Rachel's protest was lost in Luca's angry protestations.

'You should not talk of your friend that way,' he said. 'You should know she is not a woman who bed-hops indiscriminately. To suggest such a thing is…'

He broke off, apparently unable to find the English for what he needed, and finished with a stream of Italian.

Kurt's startled face made Rachel laugh, and she grasped Luca's arm as it seemed he could any minute explode into a physical fury against Kurt.

'It's OK,' she explained. 'I know he's teasing.' Then she looked at Kurt. 'We haven't had a lot to joke about this morning.'

'Ah!'

'And Rachel has already been unduly upset!' Luca added, bringing not an 'ah' this time in response from Kurt but a quick frown.

'Rach?'

'I'm fine,' she said, catching his eye and silently

begging him not to pursue the subject, because she wasn't entirely sure just how fine she was.

Surely she wouldn't cry again…

Fortunately, Alex and Phil walked in at that stage, and Rachel could tell from their faces they'd heard the news.

'The baby is being transferred back to his regional hospital. He'll be cared for there for whatever time he has left,' Alex said, but his eyes were asking questions Rachel didn't want to answer.

'It was a family decision,' Luca told him, standing up and walking across to the two men, shaking hands with both of them, then remaining close by to explain. 'We spoke only to the parents, and we left them to talk to each other, then they called us back and eventually asked the inevitable question.'

'Whether we would operate if the child was ours?' Phil said, sympathy in his voice.

Luca nodded, but before he could reply, Rachel stood up.

'I answered that one,' she said, looking directly at Alex. 'I said if he was mine I would operate, but my answer wasn't an emotional one, Alex. It was nothing to do with what happened with Reece. I just pointed out how healthy little Bobbie is and said we'd operated on children who were far smaller and less well developed. I said his size and general health would make a difference in the overall result—make the risks much less—then the family arrived…'

She couldn't go on—telling Alex she'd given an unemotional reply to the question yet choking up now as she talked about it.

Though for Bobbie, she was sure, not because of the past.

'It is their decision to make and we have to respect it,' Alex said wearily, 'but, like you, Rachel, I felt he was so healthy, that little boy, he stood an excellent chance of getting through not just this op but the next two.'

'But we can't promise normal life even after all the operations, can we?' Luca said. 'And it was my impression that's the promise those parents wanted.'

The gloom in the room was palpable, but then Annie whirled in.

'OK, you lot, no operating this afternoon, so let's have a unit meeting over lunch. I've booked a table for us at the Seasalt Café down by the shore and have liberated one of the hospital minibuses to take us there.'

It was the last thing Rachel felt like doing—socialising with the others—but she knew they all needed to be jolted out of the depression that was already settling in, and put on a brave face as she congratulated Annie on her brilliant idea.

'Let's go!' she said, slinging her handbag over her shoulder and heading for the door. 'Before our usually budget-conscious unit manager changes her mind!'

The others followed her out, Kurt introducing a safe topic of conversation—food. More specifically the virtues of various brands of sea salt he'd tried while in Australia.

'He's a clever man, Kurt,' Luca said, moving smoothly through the others to walk beside her. 'He not only senses the mood of people, but can find a way to change it. Did he know Maggie is as interested in cooking as she appears to be?'

'I suppose we all know that—we've eaten at her

and Phil's place often enough. But Kurt's clever in that he thinks to change the subject. Me, I'd just have plodded gloomily along.'

'Never gloomily,' Luca contradicted. 'There is too much sunshine in your nature for you to be gloomy for long. Sad, yes, but that is different. Sad is natural. Gloomy—pah! Not you!'

He waved his hands, dismissing her gloom as ridiculous, then leant closer and whispered in her ear.

'If we sit together, may I hold your hand on the bus?'

'Like two kids at school?'

Luca smiled.

'I suppose a bit like that, but I was not thinking childish thoughts.'

'I know you weren't,' Rachel told him, but what she didn't know was how to deal with her own thoughts, let alone how to handle Luca's.

The Seasalt, to Rachel's delight, was situated on a cliff near the head of a narrow inlet, so the waves washed in beneath it, broke over the rocks in a sparkle of spray and a flurry of foam, then rolled out again, providing nature's music as an accompaniment to the meal.

'This city is so beautiful, with the beaches and the ocean close enough for us to lunch above them,' Luca said, breathing deeply to inhale the 'sea-salted' air.

The meal, too, was special, Rachel choosing a dish of squid barbecued with a chilli marinade, while Luca pronounced his grilled swordfish the best meal he'd had in Australia.

But when the plates were cleared, Annie called them to attention.

'I warned you it was a working lunch,' she said. 'As you all know, this unit was set up as a prototype of a small paediatric cardiac surgical unit, but it was always in the nature of a trial. So I thought you might like to know that the higher-ups at Jimmie's and in the Health Department are all very pleased with the way things are going, and the board of Jimmie's has just committed to keeping the unit running.'

Someone cheered and there was a general raising of glasses in a toast. Then Annie silenced them again with an upraised hand.

'But now the unit will be permanent we need to start getting things together, so the people who will be appointed when the US members of this team go back home have everything already set up for them. We're already training theatre and nursing staff, and specialist paediatric cardiac surgeons are being approached to head up the new unit. But there are little things that need doing. Up to now, we've been using information sheets Alex brought with him from the US, updated and changed to fit with Australian hospital procedures but still copies of other hospitals' info. I think we need our own, and I want help from all of you to make sure the information we give out to parents is easily understood and covers all they need to know. Not an easy task, but we'll do it.'

'I'll be revamping the surgical procedure ones,' Alex said, taking over from his wife. 'And Phil is doing general information on congenital heart disease. Maggie, I'd like you and Kurt to work on a glossary of terms, explaining in simple English the words, phrases and acronyms parents will hear all the time.'

He paused, then turned to Rachel.

'We'll also need to revamp the information we

send home with parents—post-op care info. I'll get Susie from the PICU to do wound care and dressings and the pharmacy to do medication. Would you like to tackle feeding babies with congenital heart defects? I'll give you what I have from other hospitals, but you'll have to check with the pharmacy about supplements available here.'

He paused, then added, 'Luca, you're not obliged to do any of this, but maybe you have some suggestions for Rachel of what, in your experience, is offered to parents.'

'I'll be happy to work with Rachel on this project,' Luca said. 'And as we apparently have the bonus of a free afternoon, maybe we can start when we return to the hospital.'

He turned to smile at Rachel, who knew this wasn't nearly as good an idea as he and Alex seemed to think. She needed to be avoiding Luca, not having more opportunities for them to be together thrust upon her.

The general conversation turned to what parents needed to know. Keep it practical, Scott suggested. Keep to simple notes but with web sites and contact phone numbers of support groups so families could find out more when and if they so desired. This suggestion came from Kurt, who had designed an information pamphlet on the bypass machine that was now used in many hospitals throughout the US.

Rachel began to think about what she knew about feeding. Babies with congenital heart disease grew more slowly than healthy babies, and those with congestive heart failure, as a result of their defect, might grow in length but put on weight very slowly.

'They need a greater caloric intake, because their

hearts have to work so hard, yet they usually take in less food because they breathe rapidly and are more easily fatigued.'

As Luca spoke, Rachel knew they were on the same wavelength. Papers on feeding infants with congenital heart disease would be available in every large hospital in the world, but she understood Annie's desire to have one specifically designed for the unit here at Jimmie's. But to work with Luca on it?

Not ideal!

'It was a good idea of Annie's, taking everyone to lunch,' Luca said, when he'd followed Rachel off the bus and they were re-entering the hospital. 'And to have a job to do—that, too, will take people's minds off the baby.'

Rachel nodded but he sensed she was distracted, and he wondered if mentioning the baby had been a mistake.

But when she turned to him and asked, 'Do you think Annie asked us to work together because she thinks there's something going on between us?' he realised how far off the track his assumption had been.

'Would that bother you? For people to think this?'

She looked at him, amber eyes serious, scanning his face as if to commit his features to memory.

'I don't know,' she finally replied, and he knew from the little frown creasing her forehead that she spoke the truth.

He smiled at her.

'Maybe we shall have to test it out. Get something going on between us so you can see if people knowing worries you.'

For a moment he thought he'd lost her, then she

smiled, not only with her lips but with her eyes as well.

'Maybe we shall,' she said softly, and Luca felt his body respond, not to the smile but to the implication in her words.

This was not the time, however, so he set it aside, sitting at her desk with the folder of information pamphlets Annie had collected on feeding infants with heart problems.

'Let's read them all, mark the pieces we think are excellent, and take notes about what we don't like.'

Rachel handed him a small pile of maybe ten information sheets and folded pamphlets.

'Half each!'

They read, but Luca found his attention wandering, and he wondered if Rachel was as aware of his body beside her as he was of hers.

'Pooh! Too much information in most of these,' she said some time later, setting the last of her pile aside. 'I wonder if we're trying to generalise too much. Maybe we should have a computer program with a variety of options, and printout sheets according to specific needs. Say, infants awaiting surgery who need to be built up to a certain weight. Their needs are different to a neonate post-operatively and different again to a two-year-old who's had a minor adjustment to a shunt. Then we've got babies who've come off the ventilator and don't take kindly to oral feeding—there's such a wide range of patients.'

'Special printouts are an excellent idea,' Luca said, 'and so is dinner. Do you realise everyone else has gone home? We are the last two here.'

She looked around in disbelief, and Luca laughed.

'Did you really not hear people say goodbye to you? People leaving?'

Rachel shook her head.

'I'm very good at focussing,' she said, and he knew she must be. To have continued working in Theatre with babies with heart defects when her own baby had died of a similar condition, it would have required a tremendous effort of divorcing her work from her emotions—tremendous focus.

'Then could you now focus on food,' he suggested. 'I know I had a good lunch, but my stomach is thinking seriously of dinner.'

Keep it light, Luca's head warned, and he smiled at her.

'If we're to check out if it worries you that people think there is something going on, what better way to get started than to eat together? We can talk about the papers or computer program we will prepare. Besides, when Kurt left he said he was going to visit some friends, so he'll not be waiting for you at home.'

He paused, then, sensing hesitation, pressed on.

'Think of it as colleagues sharing a work-related meal.'

She looked startled and he realised he'd kept it too light.

'Is that all you want us to be? Colleagues?'

His heart seized with something that felt very like panic, then he saw the little smile playing on her lips and was able to breathe again. But he still took a few seconds to slow his pulse before answering.

'No, it is not,' he said, and he leaned towards her and kissed her on the lips. 'And you know that very well, my lovely Rachel. But I have promised not to rush you.'

Was one more very gentle kiss rushing things?

Perhaps not for she kissed him back, tentatively at first, but soon her lips firmed as if they wanted to take equal responsibility for the pleasure they were sharing.

Then she drew away.

'It's about trust,' she said, and he'd learned enough about her to know what she meant.

'I can understand trust is hard for you when your first husband left you the way he did,' Luca said. 'But it's also about attraction, surely. The attraction is there for both of us—a strong attraction, Rachel. Can we not just follow our instincts with it and see where they lead us?'

'Straight to bed,' she teased, smiling at him, though her eyes were still wary. 'But then what happens? In four weeks' time you fly back to Italy and that's it?'

She smoothed her fingers across his jaw-line, a tentative exploration, then tried to explain.

'I know I can't expect commitment—who could in such a short time?—but...'

'But you are afraid you will be hurt again.'

Luca put his arms around her and drew her close, kissing her cheek, her temple, pressing his lips against her forehead.

'Believe me when I say I wouldn't hurt you for the world. Trust me on that, Rachel. If, in four weeks' time, our relationship has developed to the stage where we believe it has a future, that will be a cause for happiness, not pain. And if it hasn't developed that way, then there'd be no pain.'

She drew away, studied him for a moment, then this time she initiated the kiss, whispering, 'I guess not,' as her lips closed on his.

'Uncomfortable,' she said at last, drawing away from him again. 'Not an ideal kissing position, sitting side by side on office chairs.'

'I can think of an ideal position back at my place,' Luca said, pushing her hair back from her face and tucking stray bits of it behind her ears so he could better see her clear skin and fine features.

'I can guess where,' she said, smiling as she touched a finger to his lips. 'But I think you mentioned being hungry. Perhaps we should eat first and discuss positions afterwards.'

Excitement pulsed through Luca's blood, certain of the promise in Rachel's words.

'Let me take you somewhere special,' he said. 'You have been in Sydney for, what, five months? You must know the best places where we can have a sumptuous meal.'

Her smile slipped a little, and she shook her head.

'I don't need fancy courting, Luca,' she said. 'And I'm not much good in "the best" restaurants.' She used her fingers to make inverted commas. 'I like the local places, where I feel at home.'

He understood what she was saying, but not why it made her look sad. He wanted to ask, but one thing he'd learned about Rachel was that if he asked, she'd probably tell him, and he wasn't entirely sure he wanted to know the answer.

'We shall go to the Italian place again?'

She shook her head.

'Half the team will be there, and the other half will probably be at the Thai place on the other side of the park. But there's a Spanish restaurant not far down the road from where we live. It's further from the hospital so the others haven't discovered it—or maybe they don't like Spanish food. Kurt and I go there sometimes—or I go on my own if he's busy. It's run by a lovely family—they make you feel as if you're a guest in their house, rather than someone visiting a restaurant.'

An anxious look, then she added, 'Do you like Spanish food?'

'I love it,' Luca assured her. 'We shall go there, then after eating we can walk back to our temporary homes.'

He stood up, and held her chair while she, too, stood, then, because she was so close he touched her, and they kissed again. But this time, their bodies touching, the kiss grew more impassioned. Luca drew her even closer, fitting her soft, slim litheness hard against his body, knowing she'd feel his arousal—wondering how she might react.

With encouraging fervour, he realised, and, as lust banished hunger from his mind, the practical Italian he claimed he was wondered what there was to eat in his refrigerator.

Nothing Spanish, that's for sure.

'You're buzzing.'

The words, whispered against his lips, were, coming from Rachel, totally unexpected, but he met the challenge.

'In every cell,' he told her, smiling as he kissed her once again.

Rachel chuckled but drew away from him.

'Not your body, your pager. It's in your pocket. I could feel it vibrating.'

'*Dio!* I should have turned it off.'

His fingers fumbled as he dragged the demanding little machine from his pocket.

'Could you do that?' Rachel asked. 'Turn it off?'

He looked at her and hesitated, then went for the truth, though he'd lost one woman from his life by his commitment to his job and his refusal to be out of touch with his workplace.

'No. I never have been able to,' he admitted, and was relieved to see her smile.

'I can't either,' she said, 'and I can hear mine buzzing in my handbag.'

Luca was already dialling the number when Rachel looked at her own pager and confirmed it was Alex wanting them.

'Hospital, a.s.a.p.,' he said when he answered. 'The Archers have changed their minds but they want the op done now. Mr Archer spoke to me. He says his wife can't stand the strain of waiting any longer, and if we leave it until tomorrow, Bobbie would have to go into the queue after the other operations.'

'I understand,' Luca told him. 'Rachel and I are still at the hospital. I'll get her something to eat while she prepares the theatre and we'll both be ready when you wish to start.'

'Good. Maggie's on her way to do the pre-op stuff so she'll be there before too long. I have to round up Kurt and some theatre staff. See you shortly.'

'You'll get me some food?' Rachel said.

'You are surprised I would do that? Because I'm practical, or that I care enough to make sure you have something to eat before you have to stand in Theatre for many hours?'

Her soft chuckle rippled in the air between them.

'Both, I guess. I'm not used to someone looking after me. Apart from Kurt, and though he cooks because he loves it, he'd go without food for days if he was thinking of other things.'

Luca looked pleased with her answer, and as Rachel followed him out of the room, she sensed their relationship had shifted more in that small interchange than it had in the heated kisses they'd exchanged.

Relationship? Where had that word come from? OK, she was coming to terms with the attraction, but relationships were a whole other ball game…

And the conversation they'd had earlier—when he'd asked her where they should eat—had reminded her of the huge gap between their lives.

No, for all Luca's talk of trust there was no way whatever happened between them could be anything but a brief affair.

She walked into the theatre, turning on lights, her mind switching from personal matters to work, but, in spite of her common-sense reading of the situation, there was a warm fuzzy feeling inside her that she hadn't felt for a long time. As if the ice around her heart might finally be melting.

Now, *that* was a dangerous thought.

'Work!' she told herself, and set about checking the preparations that had been done earlier, and not disturbed because much the same things would have been needed for their morning list.

Blood. Maggie would see to that. Fluids, drugs, spare drapes, spare swabs…

CHAPTER SIX

'I JUST love working with you guys.' Ned had arrived. 'Halfway through a delicate negotiation with a chick from A and E, and the pager buzzes. It's enough to give a man a heart attack, and I think, well, all's lost now with this woman, but, no, she thinks I'm just the greatest—having a pager and being on call for paediatric heart surgery. I tell you, Rachel, I've gone up so far in her estimation, it'll be straight to bed next date.'

'Men!' Rachel said. 'You shouldn't talk like that— not about any woman.'

'Hey, I was joking. I've been taking Katie out for ages now, and we were cooking dinner, not really having sex.'

'Who was not having sex?'

Luca came in at the exact moment Rachel was wondering if she'd scolded Ned because her own passionate kiss-fest had been interrupted.

'None of us tonight,' Ned said gloomily. 'I don't know about you, Rachel, but I come out of these operations seriously whacked.'

'It's the emotional strain on top of physical tiredness,' Rachel told him, in softer tones. 'Much as we try to pretend it isn't a tiny infant on the operating table, we can't entirely divorce ourselves from the facts. And it's human nature that babies and children grab our hearts in ways older people don't.'

'Because they are so helpless,' Luca said, then he

changed the subject. 'I brought a meal for you. It is in the lounge. Will you have coffee?'

Rachel glanced around the theatre, checking again that all was in readiness.

'Yes, please,' she said, then crossed to check the trolley that held spares of everything the surgeons could possibly need.

'That's pretty nice, a doctor getting food for a theatre nurse,' Ned said. 'The guy sweet on you?'

Sweet on me, or looking for a pleasant sexual liaison for the four weeks he's in Sydney? For all Luca's talk of trust, Rachel still didn't know, but the big problem was that she wasn't sure she cared...

In fact, an affair without emotional entanglements might be just what she needed to finally get over Jake and his defection.

With an affair, there'd be no need to worry about the future—no question of having children...

'I don't think so,' she said to Ned, but he'd obviously decided she wasn't going to answer and had left the theatre.

She followed him out, but to the lounge not the changing rooms. Luca was right—she needed something to eat before the operation started. During lengthy daytime ops, they always had extra staff on hand to take over so the main staff could take a coffee-break, but not tonight. Tonight the team was on its own.

'It's not Spanish food, but I hope it will be good,' Luca said, putting a steaming cup of coffee beside the plate of food. He looked anxiously at Rachel then added, 'I can't stay and talk while you eat. Alex has asked me to do the opening with Scott so I'd better change.'

'You're excused, then,' Rachel joked, but she wasn't sure she should be joking, for his face, as he walked away, was very serious. It had been an odd thing for Luca to do. Mind you, it had been odd for a man to even think of getting a meal for her, but to apologise for not sitting with her while she ate?

Maybe it was Italian politeness—not letting someone eat alone.

Once again she felt the gulf that stretched between them—not only the difference in their financial status she'd felt earlier when he'd talked of fancy restaurants, but the cultural differences between them.

Though that shouldn't matter. Not if all that happened between them was a pleasurable affair.

Now *she* felt unaccountably serious…

Bobbie Archer came through the op like a little champ. So often, when Alex switched a baby from the pump to fending for itself, there was a time when the heart had to be operated manually, either the surgeon's or Rachel's fingers squeezing it gently to simulate its normal action and remind the little organ what it was supposed to do. But this time, while the team held their collective breath, the heart began to pump immediately and a cheer went up from the tired men and women who were present in the quiet theatre.

'He'll do well,' Luca said, as he, Kurt and Rachel walked home together a little later. Phil and Maggie would remain at the hospital overnight, but all the signs were good, and there was a feeling of contentment among the medical staff who had worked to save Bobbie's life.

'He will,' Kurt agreed, 'but in such a short time

he'll need another op then, in a couple of years, the third. It must put a tremendous strain on the family, to be getting him better, then having to see him go downhill again with each op.'

'I would like to help those parents,' Luca said. 'Do they get help from the government? From church organisations? I know their worry was the cost to the other members of their family—do they have in Australia financial support for people like the Archers?'

'I don't know,' Rachel said. 'I know there are support groups similar to the ones we have in the States, but I've never enquired about financial support.'

'We should look into it,' Luca said, and again she felt the warmth she'd experienced earlier, as if Luca including her in this project was special in some way.

'But you can't help all the families who are financially strapped,' Kurt pointed out. 'No one person could.'

'No,' Luca agreed, 'but do you ever read the stock-market reports? Which companies are among those making the most profits? Pharmaceutical companies, that's who. We use their products, we help make them their huge profits, so why should they not give back more to the patients we serve?'

'I think most of them donate to research,' Rachel suggested, although she wasn't entirely sure.

Luca gave a snort of derision.

'And take the money back as contributions to their own research scientists in some cases. But you are right, they do give in some areas. What we need is to wheedle some money out of them to go into a fund to provide financial support where it is needed.'

He nodded decisively and Rachel realised he was no longer thinking of the Archers.

Something he confirmed when he said, 'I must see if I can set it up in conjunction with my own clinic.'

My own clinic? The guy owned a clinic? And as he was into hearts, then it would undoubtedly do cardiac surgery—the highest income-earner for hospitals in the US.

No wonder Alex knew the man was wealthy.

Again the difference in their status struck home and Rachel was glad Kurt was with them. In spite of the physical attraction between them—or perhaps because of it—she needed to think things through a bit more thoroughly before getting deeper into a relationship with Luca.

What if she fell in love with him?

Truly and deeply in love?

It was one more thing to worry about on top of her unwillingness to get involved because of the past...

She'd known from other things he'd said that he was from a different world to hers—different in more ways than language and culture—and while Cinderella had married her prince, Rachel doubted her foot would fit Luca's glass slipper.

They had reached the building where she and Kurt lived, and she echoed Kurt's goodnight, putting out her hand to shake Luca's. In the glow cast by the streetlight she saw his disappointment, but he took her hand, shook it politely and added his own goodnight.

'I thought you guys had advanced at least as far as goodnight kisses,' Kurt said as Luca walked away. 'I was going to do a ''vanishing quickly into the building'' act so you'd have some privacy.'

'Don't bother on my account,' Rachel snapped at him, though Kurt wasn't to blame for the situation.

He must have sensed her mood, for he put his arm around her as they climbed the stairs to the third floor.

'Love's a bitch, isn't it?' he said gently, and Rachel nodded.

'Not that I'm in love with him,' she hurried to point out.

'Yet!' Kurt said, echoing her own unhappy thoughts. 'Tell me at least you're attracted to him. How could you not be? He's a seriously attractive man.'

'And a seriously wealthy one. He owns a clinic! And from the way he spoke, that's the equivalent of a small, private, specialist hospital back home. You know how much money those places make. And to set it up would have cost a bomb!'

They reached their landing and Kurt unlocked the door of their flat.

'Can't see yourself in the role of Cinderella?' he teased, though his eyes were full of sympathetic understanding.

'With these feet?' Rachel said, lifting one of her normally sized feet for his inspection.

'Maybe glass slippers come in larger sizes,' Kurt suggested, heading for the kitchen to fill the kettle.

'Then the ugly stepsisters would have fitted their feet in,' Rachel reminded him, then she said no to his offer of a coffee, wished him goodnight and headed for bed. It had been a long and stressful day, made more stressful, not less, by what had been, until recently, a peaceful walk home.

*   *   *

Bobbie Archie continued to do well. Rachel knew this from personal experience, as she'd been drawn, for the first time in years, to the PICU so she could see the baby for herself. Her visits there became so regular Mrs Archer now treated her as a friend, showing her photos of her other children and chatting on about them.

Children!

For the first time in four years Rachel considered— rationally—the possibility of having other children herself. After all, if she was done with non-involvement, might not children be somewhere in her future?

But to lose another baby?

Go through that pain?

She wasn't sure it would be possible…

Luca had been with the Archers the day after the op—the first time she'd peered through the glass windows into the small room to see how Bobbie was faring. Luca had brought in another chair and had been sitting in front of the couple, talking earnestly.

Offering them money?

The thought had made her feel slightly ill, though she'd known the Archers desperately needed help. But it was yet another reminder of Luca's wealth that had churned inside her.

He'd glanced up and seen her, immediately excusing himself to the couple and coming out.

'It is you who should be in there,' he said, studying her as if to gauge if she could take the emotional fallout. 'They were thanking me for explaining things—apologising for their back-flip and saying how your words kept coming back to them. It changed their minds—the things you said about giving Bobbie a chance.'

'I don't think I need to talk to them again,' Rachel told him, mainly because her heart, which she'd thought she'd brought under control with reminders about the difference in her and Luca's respective lives, was behaving very badly, and a return to her non-involvement policy—with babies and with men—suddenly seemed a very good idea.

'But they want to thank you,' Luca protested, warm brown eyes smiling persuasively down at her.

'I was only doing my job,' Rachel told him, and she walked away. But later in the day she returned, drawn to the beautiful little boy, and so the friendship began, and thoughts of having babies sneaked back into her heart.

Not Luca's babies, of course.

She was telling herself this as she walked to work a few days after Bobbie's operation. She was on her own, as she wanted to get there early and Kurt was still in bed. Today's list was long, and although some of the operations they'd perform were only minor, she still had to see all was in readiness, not just for the first procedure but for all the ensuing ones.

Luca, standing at his window and looking out at the sun rising over the ocean, saw her leave her apartment building. Something had come between them in the last few days. One day the woman had been kissing him with such passion it would surely have led to bed, then suddenly she had withdrawn, talking, joking with him, but with an invisible barrier erected between them.

Did she regret telling him of her child who died? Or had her involvement with Bobbie brought back thoughts of her ex-husband, who maybe, in spite of her protestations, she still loved?

Even from this height he could see the easy way she walked, and he could picture her face, lifted to the wind that blew pink petals from the flowers on the trees that lined the road. But who could understand women? He had enough problems with Italian women, in spite of growing up with four sisters, but American women—sometimes it seemed they were a different species altogether.

Yet he knew enough of Rachel to know he wanted her—physically, more than any woman he'd ever met.

Beyond that? He had no idea, apart from the fact that she'd be an asset to his clinic. Was that a better reason to be pursuing her than lust?

Surely it was. It had substance, and purpose and practicality all going for it, though a squirmy feeling in his guts suggested a woman might not see it in the same light.

Especially a woman like Rachel.

She disappeared around a bend in the road, and he walked away from the window. It was time to shower and dress and go to work himself.

'Will you do the PDA on Rohan Williams?'

Luca turned to find Alex behind him, about to enter the rooms they all shared.

'Of course. I have his notes. Will Scott assist?'

'Scott and Phil,' Alex told him, 'but I thought you might like to take the lead.'

'I would indeed,' Luca said, proud that he was considered enough of the team to take this position in a procedure—albeit a simple one.

He realised it might not be quite so simple when

he saw the theatre crammed with medical students and knew he'd have to explain every move he made.

'Not afraid of operating with an audience, are you?' Rachel whispered to him, her eyes alight with glee, the barrier he'd sensed apparently lowered for the duration of the operation.

'More afraid of operating so close to you,' he murmured back, so only she would hear him. 'Such proximity between us can be very dangerous.'

He knew she was smiling behind her mask, and he felt a surge of hope that everything would be all right between them once again.

Then his mind leapt ahead, taking a giant stride as it conjectured that maybe one day this could be their life—working together to save the lives of infants. He hauled back on this flight of fancy. It was enough that Rachel was teasing him again!

'I'm sure you all know,' he said, addressing the students while Phil made the initial incision, 'that the ductus arteriosis is a small duct between the aorta and the pulmonary artery that allows the maternal blood in a foetus to travel all around the body. This duct will normally close soon after a baby starts breathing.'

Someone, presumably a lecturer with the group, had flashed up a diagram of a heart on the wall, with arrows showing normal blood flow and the small hole of the duct between the arteries.

'Sometimes the duct doesn't close, and we have to do it. The echo will show you more of what we need to do.' Kurt was in charge of the echocardiogram machine and he manipulated the probe so a picture of Rohan's heart, as small as a green peach, was flashed on another screen in the state-of-the-art theatre.

'You will see it does not have clean lines like the

drawing, but ligaments and blood vessels attached to it, and the pericardiac sac around it—plenty of areas for a mistake. So, first, after opening the pericardium and using small stitches to hold it in place—temporarily, of course—against the ribs so we get a good view, we separate out the tissues until we can clearly see the two arteries.'

He was good, Rachel realised as she worked beside him as lead surgeon for the first time. His movements were neat and sure—no hesitation, no fumbling.

But it was a relatively simple operation and, explaining every move, Luca completed it, then as Phil sewed up the incision, Luca gave the students a talk on how important sutures were, and how, by placing them precisely, at an exact distance apart, the surgeon gave the wound a better chance of healing without infection and, as a result, minimised any scarring.

'You talk about me teaching!' Rachel said to him when she caught up with him in the changing room late in the morning. 'You handled those kids brilliantly. Do you deal with a lot of students in your clinic?'

Luca, who, fortunately for Rachel's peace of mind, was fully dressed, grinned at her.

'I don't have a clinic yet,' he said. 'Well, I have a clinic building, and some staff already appointed, and even a waiting list for procedures when I return and the clinic opens officially, but I have lectured students in hospitals were I worked and trained, and I enjoy imparting what I know to them. Especially the ones who are eager to learn—they are a delight to teach.'

Rachel smiled to herself at his enthusiasm. Only a good teacher would enjoy his students so much. She would have liked to know more about the clinic as well—would have liked to ask—but she held back. She'd managed to put a little distance between herself and Luca over the last few days—mainly by avoiding him as much as possible, using the excuse of visiting Bobbie to not walk home with him and Kurt.

Surely she wasn't going to be tempted back to a closer relationship just because the man was a good teacher and surgeon? Surely the less she knew about Luca the better.

She showered and changed, intending to walk back to her flat for lunch, knowing the exercise would get the kinks out of her body and relax her muscles before the afternoon session.

Had Luca guessed her intention that she saw him just ahead of her on the pathway leading out of the hospital?

Two choices. Walk behind him all the way back to their separate apartments and be acutely embarrassed if he turned for some reason and saw her stalking him.

Or call his name.

She called his name.

'You're going home?' he asked, slowing his pace so she could catch up with him.

'I often do when we have two sessions in Theatre in one day. I find the fresh air clears my head and the walk helps me unstiffen.'

'Unstiffen—I like that word.'

Relief helped the unstiffening process. They were going to have a nice, neutral, non-involvement conversation. The distance she'd cultivated so carefully would remain!

'I'm not sure it is a word,' Rachel admitted. 'But it does describe what I feel I need. It's not that I'm tense during operations—well, not during most of them—but my joints seem to seize up and I need a brisk walk to shake them loose.'

Luca laughed and put an arm around her shoulders.

Casual as it was, it still did away with the nice, neutral, non-involvement idea.

Maybe not from his side, but the heat skating along her nerves with silken insistence certainly had ruined it from her side.

Would a wild romp in bed with Luca unstiffen all her joints as effectively as walking?

Unstiffen something, she thought irreverently, then she chided herself for such an earthy thought.

What was happening to her, that sex was so often in the forefront of her mind?

Sex and babies, though of the two, the 'babies' part was infinitely more scary!

Could she put it down to the long period of time where there'd been none of either in her life—when she'd avoided babies like the plague and hadn't felt even mildly interested in a physical relationship?

And, forgetting babies, could that be nothing more than a build-up of frustration, though she was reasonably sure she hadn't felt frustrated?

'Is it such a puzzle you are contemplating?' Luca asked, when they reached the entrance to her building. She turned to him, eyebrows raised in query.

'You are frowning—almost fiercely. I'm hoping I'm not the cause.'

'Only in part,' Rachel told him, smiling because it was the truth. For whatever reason, she was attracted to Luca—in fact, there had to be a stronger word than attracted, though she couldn't think of it. And if the operation on Bobbie Archer hadn't been called for that evening when they'd kissed, she knew there was a ninety-nine point nine per cent chance they'd have ended up in bed.

And if that had happened, she'd no longer have been frustrated, and that would no longer have been a reason for how she was feeling.

Luca was watching her as if trying to read her thoughts, and she was glad he couldn't because if they didn't make sense to her, they certainly wouldn't make sense to him.

Play The *Lucky Hearts* Game

and get...
FREE BOOKS & a FREE GIFT...
YOURS to KEEP!

Yes! I have scratched off the silver card. Please send me my **FREE BOOKS** and **FREE MYSTERY GIFT**. I understand that I am under no obligation to purchase any books as explained on the back of this card. I am over 18 years of age.

Scratch Here!
then look below to see
what you can claim...

M5II

Mrs/Miss/Ms/Mr _____ Initials _____

BLOCK CAPITALS PLEASE

Surname _____

Address _____

_____

Postcode _____

Twenty-one gets you
4 FREE BOOKS and a
MYSTERY GIFT!

Twenty gets you
1 FREE BOOK and a
MYSTERY GIFT!

Nineteen gets you
1 FREE BOOK!

TRY AGAIN!

The Reader Service™ — Here's how it works:

Accepting your free books places you under no obligation to buy anything. You may keep the books and gift and return the despatch note marked "cancel." If we do not hear from you, about a month later we'll send you 6 brand new books and invoice you just £2.75* each. That's the complete price — there is no extra charge for postage and packing. You may cancel at any time, otherwise every month we'll send you 6 more books, which you may either purchase or return to us — the choice is yours.

*Terms and prices subject to change without notice.

THE READER SERVICE™
FREE BOOK OFFER
FREEPOST CN81
CROYDON
CR9 3WZ

NO STAMP
NECESSARY
IF POSTED IN
THE U.K. OR N.I.

CHAPTER SEVEN

THEY talked of the operation as they walked, and of Bobbie Archer's progress, but beneath the conversation something else was going on. Like sub-titles in a foreign film, Luca's body spoke to hers, and for all she tried to stop it, her body responded.

'Well, here we are. I'm off upstairs for a quick peanut butter and jelly sandwich.'

Luca's face showed such disgust she had to laugh.

'It's comfort food,' she said to him.

'And you need comfort?' His voice, deep and husky, and his eyes, suddenly hot with desire, told her just what manner of comfort he was offering.

'Not that kind of comfort,' she said, though her heart was beating erratically, and her breath coming fast and shallow. 'Peanut butter and jelly—they're reminders of home, and childhood—of simple things and simpler times when I didn't know beautiful children like Reece and Bobbie could be born with heart defects.'

'I, too, like simple things,' Luca said, and Rachel hesitated. Should she invite Luca into her house? The fairy-tale that still fluttered around in her thoughts switched from Cinderella to Red Riding Hood, and though Luca was no wolf, he nonetheless represented danger.

'Well, peanut butter, jelly and bread are the only things I know for sure we have in the pantry. Some days the refrigerator harbours cheese and ham and fruit, but on other days its shelves are bare, apart from mystery objects sprouting hairy blue mould.'

'I need to collect some papers from my apartment,' Luca said, and Rachel laughed.

'Very subtle! In that case, I'll see you later.'

'You will indeed,' Luca promised, then he leaned forward and kissed her on the lips. Rachel felt a tremor of desire begin, not at the point of contact with Luca's lips, but deep inside her belly.

A barely heard whimper of need fluttered from her lips. Luca drew her close, hugged her tight, then stepped away.

'It's as well you only had peanut and jelly to offer. Had I come inside we might not have wasted time on food. I'll meet you back here in twenty minutes, and we will walk decorously back to the hospital together.'

He smiled and touched a finger to her lips. 'So proper, though proper is not how I wish to be with you.'

It was all too much for Rachel and she moved swiftly away, amazed she hadn't melted with desire right there on the footpath.

What would a puddle of desire look like? she wondered as she climbed the steps. And if a kiss could turn her boneless, what would making love with Luca do to her?

Oh, dear!

She unlocked her door and stepped into the flat. With her knick-knacks scattered around and Kurt's jazz musician posters on the walls, it should have felt like home, but it still had the soulless feeling of rented space—of a temporary abode too long inhabited by people passing through.

Was that what she was doing? Physically, she was making a sandwich—and, having found a fresh tomato, using that instead of comfort food—but was she just passing through life? Had the death of Reece and Jake's defection turned her into an onlooker in life rather than a participant?

It was a sobering realisation, and though she argued she actively participated in work and work-related matters, she knew as far as her social life went, it was true.

'So?' she asked herself as she walked back down the stairs.

The word echoed in the stairwell but no one answered—the ghosts of those other people who'd passed through before her not offering any advice at all!

Luca watched her walk out the front door. Long-limbed and lithe, she moved with an unconscious grace that he knew was as much a part of her as breathing. He also knew if he complimented her on it, she would be embarrassed rather than pleased.

He had dated American women before, and had not found them so different, but this one? At times it seemed she was from another planet, not just another country.

She did not like compliments or fancy restaurants and though she had kissed him with such passion—or perhaps because of it?—she then changed and held him some way apart, so he had no idea whether his pursuit was gaining ground or losing it.

'You move beautifully, gracefully.'

'Crikey!' she said, then she laughed.

'I knew you would laugh if I told you,' Luca muttered at her. 'Why are you so afraid of compliments? I wouldn't offer false praise, but I see your grace and it feels right to speak of it.'

She turned towards him and he could see her embarrassment not only in a high wash of colour on her cheekbones but in her expressive eyes as well.

'I'm sorry, but I'm not used to people telling me things like that. I don't know how to react.'

He took her hand and brought it to her lips.

'You smile at me, and you say, "Thank you, Luca." Is that so hard?'

'No, I guess not, but if I accept your compliment—that I walk gracefully—I know for sure the next thing I'm going to do is trip over something and make a complete fool of myself. I'm not good at this stuff, Luca.'

She had walked on and he kept pace with her.

'Then let me teach you,' he suggested.

Silence, though he felt her body tense, and he knew she was thinking of lessons of another kind—as he was all the time when he was with her. Though they would teach each other in the bedroom—he was not vain enough to think otherwise.

Then she smiled and he felt as if the sun had come out from behind clouds. Such a cliché, he thought, but what other way to describe a feeling that made the day brighter and his body warmer?

'OK,' she said, and he knew she understood the implications of both his suggestion and her own reply. Their relationship had moved in the right direction at last!

But the afternoon was tough, and the final operation on an eighteen-month-old boy with coarctation of the aorta—a significant narrowing of the body's main artery, preventing blood circulating properly through the body—became complicated when Phil, who was operating, discovered the little patient's body had produced subsidiary vessels in an attempt to fix the problem and, rather than just removing the narrow part of the aorta and rejoining the ends, he had to find out where the new vessels led before he could move them.

'Damn, that's a coronary artery we've cut, Scott, not a subsidiary,' Phil said, as blood spurted everywhere.

'I'll sew it up,' Luca said calmly, 'while you continue with what you are doing, Phil.'

But the coronary arteries supplied the heart muscle with the blood they need to keep pumping, and without that blood the heart grew sluggish. Rachel could see the little organ swelling as blood collected within it.

'Damn!' Phil said again, while Rachel gently squeezed the bloated heart to help it pump.

Luca, she knew, would be sewing swiftly, reconnecting the two ends of the severed artery neatly and efficiently. This was what being part of a team was all about.

But the stress level had risen and when they were finally done, they all suffered let-down.

'We need better information before we cut,' Alex said later, when the team was gathered in the lounge after the final operation. They were all still in various degrees of theatre garb, as a caffeine fix had seemed more important than a shower.

'Better echo pictures,' Rachel said. 'Surely subsidiary vessels that size would have shown up in echocardiograms.'

'They should have,' Phil said, 'but when you think of the maze of vessels running around, into and out of a baby's heart, it's a wonder we get as much information as we do.'

'You're right,' Alex said, 'but maybe in future we should try to build a model of the situation so we've a three-dimensional representation of what we'll find before we get in there.'

'We don't have time for model-building in most situations,' Phil reminded him.

'And with patients like that baby—Andrew, wasn't he?—most of the information we had to hand was from the transferring hospital.'

'I know, but we still have to do better.'

Alex turned to Luca.

'In your clinic will you have your own specialist radiologist—an echocardiologist—so you can ask for the pictures you want?'

'He's already appointed and, like me, is currently expanding his knowledge, but in a hospital in London.'

'That's good,' Alex told him. 'We have our own man back home, but I'm beginning to believe to make a small unit like this work properly we need an echo-cardiologist attached to the team. He'll soon learn exactly what we need, and can do the follow-up scans on the patients and also be used in the cath lab for catheterisations. There'd be enough work.'

Alex sounded tired, although he hadn't been in Theatre for the final operation.

Luca looked around the room and realised just how much of themselves this team put into their work. It was already after eight at night, and they all still had to shower and dress and make their way home.

Although he suspected Alex would remain at the hospital until he was sure all today's patients were stable.

It was what he, Luca, would have done in the circumstances.

But these were not his circumstances, and as Alex declared a day off for the whole team for the following day, Luca glanced across at Rachel, who met his eyes and smiled.

Just a smile, but his body responded with a burst of testosterone that had his heart thudding in his chest.

Dio! He was hardly so frustrated that a smile could do this to him! Even with the promise behind the smile, he should not have been affected quite so strongly.

Was it more than lust he felt for Rachel?

Not that it was just lust—he liked her a lot. She was already, he thought, a friend.

But beyond lust?

Unable to answer any of the questions in his head, he stood up and headed for the changing rooms. He'd have a shower, dress, then walk her home. Maybe tonight they'd get to the Spanish restaurant. It was sure to be open late.

And after that, with a free day ahead tomorrow—well, who knew?

More excitement stirred and he hurried to the showers.

Rachel sat in the lounge while the team filtered out, timing their moves for when they thought the showers would be free.

Kurt, who'd followed Luca out, returned, all shiny clean and with the air of a man with fun on his mind.

'Don't expect me home,' he said to Rachel, bending to drop a kiss on her head. 'And if you've got an ounce of sense, you won't be home tonight either.'

Rachel looked up at him, and saw concern as well as mischief in his eyes.

'I'm scared about this,' she told him, and he sat down on the couch beside her and put his arm around her shoulders.

'Of course you are. You're practically a virgin, for all you've been married and had a baby. And you've still got all the old hang-ups in your head. Will he still respect me in the morning, and all that rubbish. Forget it, Rach, and go into it to have fun. Think pleasure and enjoyment. You're not Cinderella. You've got a full and rewarding life, so you don't need rescuing from the kitchen, but you do need some relaxation.'

Rachel laughed.

'I guess that's one way of putting it, but aren't there deep-breathing techniques for relaxation? Or I could take up yoga.'

'You know what I mean,' Kurt growled at her. 'And if he asks you out somewhere swish to dinner, wear the black. Do not climb into your ancient jeans and that green T you're so fond of. And take that sexy black trench coat I bought you for your birthday if you need warmth, not your old, bulky knit cardigan.'

'Yes, master!' Rachel saluted him, but his words had given her confidence. OK, her jeans and the green T might give her more confidence, but the fact that Kurt cared and, knowing that whatever happened, he'd always be there for her filled her with gladness.

He kissed her cheek and departed, leaving Rachel alone in the lounge, knowing she had to shower and change back into civvies, then...

Then what? Maybe she was making mountains out of molehills—cliché central!—and Luca hadn't even waited for her.

Maybe she'd misread the sub-titles earlier and all he intended teaching her was how to accept compliments gracefully.

She stood up and walked through to the changing room, deserted now except for Maggie who, as the anaesthetist, always saw their young patients safely back to the PICU so was always last to shower and change.

'Going to do something exciting on your day off?' Rachel asked her, and Maggie nodded.

'Very exciting, as far as I'm concerned. I'm going to spend the entire day in bed. The problems we've had lately, I can't think when I last had a sleep-in, let alone a day in bed.'

Then she blushed and Rachel laughed.

'I pictured you sleeping, not doing anything else,' she hurried to assure her friend.

Maggie smiled at her.

'Well,' she admitted shyly, 'there might be a little of something else.' Then she changed the subject. 'And you? Any plans?'

Rachel felt the heat start in her abdomen and rise towards her face so she was certain her whole body was blushing.

'Nothing special,' she managed to gulp, then she dashed into the shower cubicle and turned on the taps.

*   *   *

Luca, no doubt guessing she'd eventually return to their rooms to sign off on the operation, was waiting for her there.

'You've been thinking new thoughts about the situation between us?' he said quietly. 'I said before I wouldn't rush you.'

'Second thoughts, we call them.' She was slightly put out by the ease with which he seemed to read her mind. 'I suppose I have, but you're not rushing me.'

He smiled and she felt the last resisting chips of ice around her heart melt, and her body go on full alert, her nerve-endings so attuned to him that her nipples tightened.

'I refuse to kiss you here, for if we start we may not get home. We'll eat first. You will show me your Spanish restaurant, then let the night unfold as it will.'

He waited while she tidied her desk then they left the rooms together, not touching at all, though Rachel was so sensitised to his presence that every movement he made sent tingling messages of desire through her body.

Let's forget dinner, she wanted to say, although common sense told her she needed food, but when they exited the hospital they were barely on their way to the front gate before Luca guided her into the shadow of a thick bush beside the path. He took her in his arms, and common sense was forgotten.

His kiss met and matched the urgency her body had been experiencing and she trembled in his grasp, her need so great she thought her knees might give way.

'Let's forget dinner,' she managed to whisper, though her lungs were strangling in the tightness of desire and her breath was coming in little desperate gasps.

'I have food at my apartment—beyond what we know is in your pantry. You will come there?'

Still held tightly to him in the shadows, she nodded against his shoulder. He turned her and, with his arm firmly around her waist, guided her back to the path and along the road towards his temporary home.

'I suppose we'd look silly if we ran,' Rachel said, hoping even a weak joke might break the tension.

'Extremely so,' Luca said, his arm tightening momentarily as if in appreciation of her comment. 'Especially as I'm not at all graceful in my movements.'

'But you've got great hands in Theatre,' Rachel told him, feeling one compliment deserved another then flushing when she realised the implication behind the words.

They didn't run, but it seemed no time before they were at his apartment, and Rachel, who'd imagined this might be the moment when doubts and second thoughts reared their heads, found her excitement, far from abating, had grown, and Kurt's admonition to have fun was ringing in her head.

'What a beautiful place,' she said, when Luca opened the door to the penthouse and she saw the view out across her much smaller building. To the north were the city lights and to the east the seaside suburbs, the foreshores brightly lit and the moon shining on the night-dark ocean.

'It is sufficient,' Luca said, so offhandedly she knew he was used to such luxury—to places as luxurious as this, and maybe even more so! But the difference in their lives was not going to bother her tonight. She was going into this affair with Luca with her eyes wide open. She was going to have fun!

'Champagne?'

'Why not?' she said, walking towards the kitchen where he had the fridge door open and a bottle held aloft in one hand.

'And some things to nibble on while we drink a toast.'

He handed her the bottle, and bent again to the fridge, bringing out a large plate with an array of tiny, tempting hors d'oeuvres.

The implication of this platter struck her like a blow to the head. He'd planned for her to be here. The talk of the Spanish restaurant had been just that! No doubt there was an apartment manager somewhere in this building, part of whose job was to provide whatever food a tenant wanted.

Seduction food!

Luca must have heard her thoughts, for he put the platter on the bench and took the champagne from her, placing it on the bench as well, then he pulled her to him and held her close while he explained.

'I asked the manager to organise some food for our supper—I was thinking supper, not a meal, but our hunger for each other—well, it brought us here, and it was mutual, wasn't it?'

He had tilted her head so he could look into her eyes as he asked that last question, and looking into *his* eyes—dark with sincerity—Rachel couldn't doubt him.

She smiled, and shrugged.

'I'm sorry,' she said. 'I seem to be thinking either in fairy-tales or clichés these days and the champagne and tiny nibbles—a seduction cliché if ever I saw one.'

Luca answered her smile with a warm one of his own.

'Then I shall proceed to seduce you, my beautiful Rachel. With champagne and nibbles and compliments that will make your skin glow with colour, and your eyes sparkle like bright jewels.'

He leaned forward and kissed her gently on the lips then drew away, opening the champagne, pouring out two glasses, peeling the plastic wrap from the platter and setting it in front of her.

He passed her a brimming glass, and lifted his own in salute.

'To seduction!' he teased, and Rachel felt the colour he'd spoken of heat her cheeks.

'To seduction,' she echoed, but the fun seemed to have gone out of things. She sipped the champagne—dry bubbles fizzing off her tongue—and thought back, realising that perhaps she'd harboured in her heart the thought this might be more than a seduction—realising she'd been more caught up in the Cinderella story than she'd thought she'd been!

No, it wasn't that, she decided as Luca pressed her to take from the plate a tiny biscuit with soft cheese and a strawberry topping it. She didn't want the castle, or a prince, but being with Luca, working with him, seeing him with her friends—somewhere along the line she'd fallen just a little bit in love with him, and her silly heart must have harboured thoughts of love returned.

So the seduction scenario had struck deeper than it should have, although her head knew damn well an affair was all there'd be between them.

It was also all she wanted between them, she reminded herself.

He had guided her, while her thoughts had run riot, to a couch that looked out through wide glass windows towards the view, and was over by a CD player, organising music.

He'd put the food on a coffee-table in front of her, and the champagne was in an ice bucket beside it. Soon he'd come and sit beside her and, she had no doubt, she'd be an equal partner in whatever seduction might take place. But deep inside she felt a thin layer of ice building up again around her heart, and her head chided her for her folly in letting it melt in the first place.

'You are sad now, thinking perhaps of your husband, and of the pain he caused you,' Luca murmured, settling beside her on the couch, the warmth from his body transferring to hers where their thighs touched.

'No way!' she told him, glad she could answer honestly. 'Jake's a closed book as far as I'm concerned. I realised later that I was never really in love with him.'

'I'm glad,' Luca said, taking her empty glass from her fingers and setting it on the table, 'for I don't want thoughts of him coming between us.'

He held her gently and his kiss was more an exploration than a seduction, though as his hands touched her body, feeling their way across her shoulders, neck and back, she knew it *was* seduction.

But such sweet seduction, especially now his hands had slid across her belly and circled breasts that ached for his touch. So she became a participant instead of an onlooker and through touch explored his shape— broad shoulders and the strong bones of his skull, neat ears flat against his head, soft hair as black as midnight.

She caught her breath as he brushed his thumbs

across her demanding nipples, and bit his lip—gently but with insistence—wanting more, wanting pain herself, feeling pain from frustration.

'Strong, soft and beautiful,' Luca whispered, his hands beneath her shirt now, warm on her skin. 'You are a very special woman, Rachel, and so enticing—so exciting.'

His lips, parted from hers for speech, moved to her neck, where a nibble against her pulse had her crying out in need. Then he was gone—but not gone far, simply standing up and taking her hand, helping her up off the couch and guiding her towards a bedroom.

'Where we will be more comfortable,' she heard him say, though her mind had gone AWOL and her body simply followed where he led.

The bed was the size of Texas, but she had little time to take much notice of it, for Luca was undressing her, undoing buttons, kissing and murmuring endearments against her lips as he did it—stripping away any faint strands of resistance she might have been able to muster as he stripped away her clothes.

'Beautiful—I knew you would be,' he said, when he had her naked and she stood before him, embarrassed yet somehow proud he found her beautiful. 'Now it is your turn,' he said, holding out his arms, so serious she almost laughed.

But stripping Luca, she soon discovered, was no laughing matter. His body called to hers, his skin, like satin beneath her fingertips, tempting her to press her lips against it. And if she had any doubts about his readiness for love-making, they vanished when she put her hands against the black silk of his briefs.

Desire rendered her light-headed, almost dizzy, but

then Luca was kissing her again, and together, naked and entwined, they found the bed.

'You will make the pace, remember,' he whispered, as he drew a line with his finger from her breast to the junction of her thighs. 'You'll tell me to go fast or go slow.'

'I can barely think, let alone talk,' Rachel replied, teasing him in turn. 'Let's just go with the flow.'

'Go with the flow,' Luca repeated, moving his mouth from her lips to one pebble-hard nipple and slowly teasing it to even greater excitement with the tip of his tongue.

Rachel felt herself drowning in sensation, her nerves singing with anticipatory delight, the world reduced to here and now—to this bed, and the man who was making magic in her body.

'Ah, so sweet, so giving,' he murmured, though even without the words she knew her response was delighting him.

Then touching and kissing was no longer enough, and as Luca's fingers teased her open and his exploring thumb found the tight nub of her desire, she cried out his name, and helped him slide inside, deeper and deeper until he filled her to overflowing, his movements matching hers, bringing more and more delight until she shattered into a million glittering pieces, clutching him tight, crying his name now, feeling him expand to help her explode again, only this time he cried her name, and clung to her as if he needed an anchor to keep him tethered to the earth.

'Crikey!' she managed to croak when she finally drew breath. She hoped her attempt at weak humour might hide the awe she felt at what had just occurred.

She'd just had an orgasm of truly seismic proportions—so what was she supposed to say?

Thank you?

She probably should, but right now it was all she could do to breathe and cling to the man who'd lifted her to such incredible heights.

He moved so his weight was no longer on her, but kept his arms around her, holding as tightly to her as she clung to him. His chest rose and fell as he drew in deep breaths, and for once the man who always seemed to have so many words at his command said nothing.

But the kisses he pressed on her hair and her skin were gentle—even loving—and she knew from the tremors she'd felt in his body that his satisfaction had been as great as hers.

He lifted himself on one elbow and looked down into her face, tracing her profile with his finger.

'If I get the champagne and food, will you be upset?'

She couldn't read his eyes as the only light in the room came from beyond the open door, but she could hear uncertainty in his voice.

She raised her head far enough to kiss him on the lips.

'I'll only be upset for as long as it takes you to get them,' she told him. 'Once you're back again, I'll have no reason to be upset.'

And she wouldn't, she told herself as she sat up and turned on the bedside light so she could untangle the sheet and pull it over her body to hide her nakedness.

Making love with Luca had been a revelation of just how wonderful an experience it should be, and she had every intention of enjoying it again. As often as possible over the next three weeks.

She was going to have fun and if, at the end, losing Luca meant the ice-pack would once again form around her heart, then too bad.

He returned, set the glasses on the bedside table and filled them, then sat beside her on the edge of the bed. He pressed one glass into her hands, drew the sheet down so he could see her breasts, and raised his glass to hers.

'To love between us,' he said, sipping the cold liquid then bending, his tongue still cold, to lick at first one nipple then the other.

'I'll choke to death if you do that while I'm drinking!' Rachel told him, taking a big gulp of her drink and telling herself they couldn't possibly make love again just yet.

Luca raised his head and smiled.

'I love the way you joke while we make love,' he said. 'That word you used—"crikey"—it said so much I should have echoed it.'

He sipped his drink again and this time fed her lips with the taste of champagne from his tongue, but his hands were on her breasts, and her heart was pounding.

In a couple of effortless minutes Luca had readied her for love again, and her body called to him to take it and make his magic within it once more.

'It should not be possible,' he said, taking her hand in his and guiding it to the irrefutable evidence of his readiness. 'You have potent powers, my beautiful Rachel. Too potent for resistance.'

But this time it was she who took the glass from his hand, and she who led the way along the path to their ultimate satisfaction, teasing him until he groaned with needing her, positioning herself so she took charge and brought them both to shuddering climaxes together.

CHAPTER EIGHT

RACHEL woke to find sunlight flooding the big bedroom. Beside her, Luca still slept, his bronzed back turned towards her. Memories of the night they'd spent together brought heat to all parts of her body, while concern over what might happen next stirred uneasily in her stomach.

Shower! She'd find a shower. There were sure to be two in an apartment this size, so she wouldn't have to use Luca's *en suite* and wake him with the noise she was sure to make. Once clean she'd be able to think what to do next.

Would serviced apartments this luxurious come complete with bathrobes? Putting on the clothes she'd worn to work the previous day had no appeal at all. How could she have been so totally disorganised?

Muttering to herself, she left the room, tiptoeing quietly away down a short hall to a second bedroom which, to her delight, not only had an *en suite* but the requisite towelling robe.

She showered, washing her hair in shampoo far more expensive than the brand she normally used and lavishing the body creams she found in the bathroom all over her skin.

'You smell like spring.'

Luca was in the kitchen and it was obvious that while she had revelled in the luxuries of his second bathroom he'd woken and made use of the first, for his hair was still damp and his cheeks shone with a freshly shaven look.

He was beautiful—not a good word for a man, but Rachel could find no other, especially not when her heart was racing and her lungs felt as if they'd never breathe properly again!

He was also wearing a matching bathrobe, which gave Rachel the impression she might not need clothes after all. This thought did nothing to calm her rioting pulse.

'I've ordered breakfast to be delivered for us. The least I could do as I cheated you of dinner, but I can make coffee if you'd like it while you wait. Or juice? I have orange only, but can order whatever you would like.'

He sounded strangely formal, and the skittering sensation in Rachel's heart changed to one of dread.

That was it? He was going to give her breakfast then say goodbye?

Panic attacked her and lest he guess her feelings—there'd been times she'd been sure he could read her mind—she walked away, over to the windows of the living room, pretending to take in the view of the ocean while in truth her eyes saw nothing. Or maybe her eyes saw but her brain didn't register the view, too intent on trying to work out what to do next.

Then Luca was behind her, his hands on her shoulders—strong, warm and steadying.

'You're feeling sad? Uncomfortable perhaps? Please, don't be embarrassed with me, Rachel, for we are friends, are we not? And what we shared—that was wonderful.'

His touch fired her senses but his words, which should have comforted, cooled her heating blood because, try as she might to make something more of them, they sounded like goodbye.

'I won't have breakfast. I'll put some clothes on and go home.' She could hear her voice breaking, and tried for levity. 'I've bread for toast and plenty of peanut butter and jelly.'

'You want to go?'

Luca sounded so astounded Rachel turned to look at him.

'Don't you want me to? Weren't you saying goodbye just then?'

'Saying goodbye? To the most incredible woman with whom I've ever made love? I don't want to ever say goodbye! I want to keep you by me always—preferably in my bed. We are so well matched, Rachel, why would I say goodbye?'

Rachel's misbehaving heart, which had picked up its dancing beat again when Luca had said he didn't want to ever say goodbye and had then slipped back into morose mode when he'd talked of keeping her in bed, now settled to near normal, while her head began to work again.

There was no easy answer to his question, for how did you explain gut feelings? But ignoring that, what else was going on?

An affair—that's what was going on.

Luca had left her to answer the door. Now he let in first a young man pushing a trolley laden with food, then a middle-aged woman pushing a rack on which hung a number of long, black plastic bags, no doubt covering Lucas's shirts and suits—back from the laundry.

The two new arrivals were thanked, and no doubt tipped, though Rachel had turned back to the window.

Then she heard the door shut, and Luca called her name.

He was unloading silver dishes from the trolley to the table, having pushed the rack of clothes to one side.

'We'll eat then you can see if some of the clothes from the shop downstairs fit you. I think we should spend some of our day exploring the city and I know you wouldn't want to be wearing your yesterday's clothes.'

I could have ducked home in them and changed, Rachel thought, but didn't say because curiosity about what was in the plastic bags was vying with an uncomfortable feeling that she was in danger of becoming a kept woman. Breakfast was one thing—but dressing her? That was taking on a whole different dimension!

But how to tell him?

Bluntly!

'I'm not happy with the clothes thing,' she said, coming cautiously towards the table.

Luca looked puzzled.

'I'm not trying to buy you, Rachel, merely being practical. If you don't wish to, you don't need to even look at the clothes. They're from a shop in the foyer and can all be returned.'

He spoke stiffly and she knew she'd offended him, but she'd felt…not offended exactly but definitely uneasy, so she wasn't going to apologise.

She reached the table, saw the food spread out on it and, in spite of lingering discomfort, had to laugh.

'Well, you've certainly covered all the bases,' she said, still chuckling as she saw not only crisp bacon, scrambled eggs, hash browns and pancakes, but toast, muffins, pastries and even small jars of peanut butter and jelly. 'Can you return what we don't eat as well?'

Luca looked at the woman who smiled at him across the table. With her hair still damp from the shower, and the bathrobe revealing the slight swell of one breast, she was so enticing it was all he could do to keep his hands off her. Yet she didn't seem to know it. She was edgy, and ill at ease, and he didn't know how to make things right between them again.

At least the breakfast had made her laugh.

He walked around the table and held a chair for her while she sat down, the perfume of her body so potent he could feel his own body responding.

'We must eat,' he said, sliding one hand into the opening of her robe and cupping one full, heavy breast. 'Or we won't have the energy for more love-making.'

He was practically croaking, so great was his confusion and desire, but when she tipped her head up towards him and he saw her smile, he knew it would be all right.

For now!

For the future, he had no idea, for she was so different, this woman, to any other he had known. He dropped a kiss on her drying hair and murmured her name, then walked away before he could give in to the urge to scoop her into his arms and take her straight back to bed.

'You'll help yourself to what you like?' he said, sitting down across from her.

'Anything?' she teased, and he knew from the glint in her eyes that she, too, was aroused.

'Food!' he reminded her. 'Any of the food!'

'And later?'

'There will be time for other choices.'

He breathed more easily now, certain they were over whatever had caused her uneasiness earlier. But he must tread carefully because, more and more, he was realising that this woman was important to him.

'This is wonderful,' she announced, helping herself to pancakes and syrup and bacon and coffee, and eating with a gusto that made Luca smile. 'I hadn't realised how ravenous I was.'

She finished what was on her plate then she smiled at Luca.

'Will you think me a terrible pig if I have a pastry with my second cup of coffee?'

'I will think you honest, and delightful, as I usually do,' he said, but when he saw colour sweep into her cheeks he wondered if he'd gone too far and hurried to cover his mistake.

'I know you don't like compliments, but I can't help what I feel.'

Her eyes met his, then her gaze moved across his face, studying it as he often found her doing.

'I could get used to the compliments,' she said, her voice softened, he thought, by emotion. Then she smiled a cheeky smile that made his heart race, and added, 'As long as they don't get too over the top.'

'Ah, over the top—you warned me of that the first day we met.' He smiled back at her. 'I hope I'm learning.'

She nodded, and bit into her pastry, watching him all the time. Luca thought it the most erotic action he'd ever seen.

'If you don't behave, we shall have to leave exploring Sydney for another day, and do some more exploring of each other instead,' he warned, and she laughed, a natural, whole-hearted sound that made him feel less uncertain about the situation.

As it turned out, they did both, spending the morning back in bed then, after Rachel slipped home to change, getting a cab to a part of the city called The Rocks, where old warehouses had been turned into shops and galleries. They found a restaurant that looked out over the beautiful harbour and ate while ferries carried their passengers back and forth across the water and sleek yachts cruised beneath the famous bridge.

They returned, first to Rachel's flat where, in a burst of practicality mixed with a welter of embarrassment, she shoved her toiletries and clothes for work the next day into a backpack, then left a note for Kurt.

'I'm not too good at this affair stuff,' she explained to Luca, as, her colour still high, they walked back down the stairs.

'Will it be over the top if I say it shouldn't please me but it does?'

He stopped her on the second landing and placed his hand on her shoulders, then kissed her lightly on the lips.

'To me it means I must be a bit special to you.'

So special, Rachel's heart murmured, though her lips were still. All day her love for Luca, revealed so unexpectedly the previous evening, had grown until she knew it had become a huge force in her life.

Common sense, when she could summon it, predicted hurt at the end of the 'affair', and cautioned her to hold back, but that was impossible. She was already committed and for now it was enough to enjoy the bliss of being with Luca, and the excitement and satisfaction his body could offer hers.

Back in his apartment, the rack of clothes mocked her from beside the door, and though curiosity prompted her to take a peek—to see what he'd ordered be sent up—she ignored it, refusing to let them worry her as they had earlier in the day.

'We'll go to the Spanish restaurant,' Luca announced. 'It's a favourite with you so there will be no more putting it off.'

But first they had to shower and change, which took a while—the showering part far longer than the dressing, for they showered together and discovered how erotic it could be.

'We won't be showering together in the morning,' Rachel warned Luca as he towelled her body dry. 'If we did, we'd never get to work.'

'We could wake earlier,' he suggested, nibbling at the skin on her shoulder and sending new ripples of desire through her body.

'Enough!' she said, moving away from him. 'We'll never get to the Spanish place at this rate.'

But they did, and the proprietors greeted Rachel with their usual delight. She introduced Luca and the wife clucked over him, embarrassing Rachel by praising her to Luca.

'She's as bad as my mother,' Rachel said, when the woman had bustled off to bring them drinks and menus.

'Your mother would like you to be married?' Luca asked.

'My mother wants grandchildren,' Rachel explained. 'So badly it's a wonder she hasn't adopted some married couple purely so she could be a granny to their kids.'

'But she must understand your reluctance, given what happened in the past. Is the sole responsibility for grandchildren on your shoulders? You have no siblings?'

'Two,' Rachel told him, holding up two fingers. 'Two brothers, both adventurers who are far too busy tasting all life has to offer to tie themselves to wives and children.'

'Do you feel being married and having children must necessarily be a tie?'

Their drinks arrived, giving Rachel time to study the man who'd asked the question.

And to think about the question!

Had it just been idle conversation, or was he asking something more?

Get real! she told herself. As if a man like Luca would be thinking marriage after one admittedly wonderful night in bed.

As if a man like Luca would be thinking of marriage with someone like her at all...

She answered the question anyway.

'No, I don't, though I must admit I haven't given the subject much thought. Back when I was married and pregnant I knew I'd have to keep on working because we'd have needed two incomes to start saving for a house. There were good child-care facilities at the hospital so it wouldn't have been a major problem.'

She paused, sipped her drink, then raised her shoulders and spread her arms in an I-don't-know gesture.

'Since then...'

Luca took her hand and held it on the table.

'You've not wished to think about it. But it was what? Four years ago, I think you said. You've not a met a man since who made you think about it?'

Until now! Rachel thought, but she answered no, because she *hadn't* thought about it.

And wouldn't now.

'But you would like children with a man you loved, or would being pregnant worry you? Would you worry about the same defect occurring?'

Crikey, he was persistent!

'I don't know, Luca, because I haven't thought about that either.'

She spoke too bluntly, but images of dark-eyed babies with silky black hair had suddenly popped into her head and filled her heart with longing. She reached out and touched his hand.

'That's not entirely true,' she admitted. 'Since Bobbie's operation—my involvement with him—and, to be honest, since my involvement with you, Luca, I have started to think about it—but that's all I've done. I haven't come to any conclusion, I guess because the thought of loss persists long after the pain diminishes.'

She paused then raised his hand to her lips and kissed his knuckles.

'But I owe you thanks, Luca, for at least *making* me think about it and, to that extent, releasing me from the past so I could become more than an on-looker on life,' she said softly, hoping he wouldn't notice the emotional cracks in her voice.

Maybe he had, for he squeezed her fingers then changed the subject, talking about an opal shop they'd visited at The Rocks—and where she'd refused to al-low him to buy her an expensive piece of jewellery.

'I couldn't believe the colour in the stones,' he said. 'I'll go back there to buy gifts for my mother and my sisters—they, too, will love the colours.'

A pause, then he added, 'You'll come with me and help me choose?'

'Only if you don't insist on buying me a gift as well,' Rachel warned him, pleased to find the atmosphere between them had relaxed again.

Though perhaps Luca had been relaxed all the time and it had only been her who'd grown tense with the conversation about marriage and children.

Their meal arrived, the Spanish woman having decided what they'd eat.

'She always does that,' Rachel explained. 'I know she gives the guests a menu, but whether they have the other dishes on it I don't know, because she seems to take one look at me and decide what it is I need to eat.'

'It's delicious, and I'm glad she decided, for I'd have been far less adventurous,' Luca said, spooning the soup-like stew into his mouth.

Rachel watched him, thinking of the magic that mouth had wrought on her body, feeling desire rise like a tide within her.

'I do hope I settle down when I get back to work,' she muttered, and Luca smiled, no doubt knowing exactly what she was thinking.

'You will,' he promised her. 'You're too much of a professional to be distracted from your work.'

His prediction proved true for, although Rachel's body hummed with love whenever Luca was around, she found her concentration was, if anything, sharper.

It was as if her new sensitivity made her extra-aware of everything happening around her.

The days flew by, as if the time she spent not with Luca went especially fast, while the time with him, like the following weekend, which they spent exploring Sydney and learning more about each other, went on for ever.

Monday's operating list was always short, and she finished in Theatre well before lunchtime, so she walked through to the PICU to check on Bobbie, as she did most days.

Mrs Archer greeted her with relief.

'Oh, Rachel, would you mind sitting with him for a few minutes? I promised the other kids I'd take some photos of him then realised I didn't have a camera. I know the kiosk downstairs has those little disposable ones. I'll just duck down and get one.'

Rachel was quite happy to sit with the baby she thought of as her special charge, and smoothed her finger across his soft, warm skin.

He raised his eyelids at her touch and she could swear the big, smoky blue eyes were smiling at her.

Dark-eyed babies would start off with blue eyes, too, she thought, then shook the thought away as the eyes she was looking at filled with fright. A siren was wailing through the building.

Not loud, but strident and urgent-sounding, its cry, rising and falling insistently, made the hairs on Rachel's arms stand on end.

She looked at Bobbie, thought of Luca—where was he?—then quelled the panic rising in her chest.

It's a practice drill. All you have to do is listen to the instructions. ICUs will be excluded.

Her head told her these things but her heart still

beat erratically, a jumble of emotions skittering through her body.

'Attention, please. There is no fire so do not panic, but we are experiencing a bomb scare and would like all visitors to leave the building immediately. Staff have been trained in clearing the wards, so patients should remain where they are until instructed to move by a staff member. Staff should follow evacuation procedures as practised.'

Rachel heard the words but couldn't believe them, a disbelief she saw reflected on the faces of the two sisters monitoring the patients at the desk. Then, as the message was repeated, one of them was galvanised into action, leaving the desk and poking her head into the room where Rachel hovered protectively—though no doubt ineffectively—over Bobbie.

'Have you done a fire drill? Do you know how to bag a baby on the way to the secure rooms in the basement?'

Rachel nodded. The entire team had done a fire drill soon after their arrival at the hospital, and she'd been amazed at the extensive facilities deep below the hospital grounds where all intensive-care patients could be kept on the machines that were vital to their lives.

'Then you take Bobbie,' the sister said. 'The service elevators work on generators so even in a fire they'll take you down there. They will be set automatically to stop first at the ICU floors.'

As calmly as she could, Rachel detached the bag of fluid from the drip stand and set it on Bobbie's small bed. Then she detached the heart monitor. There were monitors where they were going, and the less gear they had to carry, the better.

Then finally she unhooked him from the ventilator and attached a bag to his breathing tube so she could squeeze air into his lungs while they made the journey to safety.

'We'll be OK, kid,' she told him, though her heart was thudding and she wondered just how safe anyone could be in a world that had gone mad. To plant a bomb in a hospital? Who would do such a thing?

She stared in dismay at the innocent face of the baby in her charge, and shook her head in disbelief.

Beyond his room a couple of aides were ushering reluctant family members out of the unit, assuring them the children would be well cared for. One near hysterical woman had to be physically moved away from her baby, a large orderly treating her as gently as he could, but with a firmness that brooked no resistance.

'OK, let's go,' the sister called, when the unit was cleared of visitors. With one nurse to each small patient, they pushed the small beds out of the rooms and formed a queue out to the service elevator foyer, pressed the button and waited their turn to go down into safety.

Waited in outward calm, but were they all hiding the inner turmoil Rachel felt?

She wished she knew these staff members better. Wished she'd spent more time in the PICU!

'So many of these things are false alarms,' one of the women said, while an aide who was with them began to sob.

'If you haven't got a baby, you should get out of the building,' the sister in charge told the crying woman. 'Use the stairs and go down to ground level and then to the muster point. Our floor is muster point five—the colour's blue—out to the right of the main gate.'

The woman looked at her as if she didn't understand, then she sobbed again and turned and fled, not towards the stairs but back into the ward.

'I'd go after her, but I can't stop bagging and patients come first,' the sister said, but Rachel guessed they all felt as tense as she did, and apprehensive for the woman who hadn't gone down the stairs—worrying what might happen to her.

To them all!

But once in the deep basement, she discovered the practice sessions had proved worthwhile for though there was an air of urgency as they pushed the small beds along a wide corridor, there was no panic. Arriving at the designated safe area, they fitted the patients back to equipment with a minimum of fuss and maximum of efficiency. A doctor circulated between the groups from the different ICUs and the CCU, making sure medication was administered on time, and that all patients were closely monitored.

'Poor Mrs Archer, she'll be going nuts,' Rachel said to the nurse who was beside her.

'Someone will explain to her—and we couldn't bring the parents down here as well—look how crammed we are as it is. Far better to have people here who can be useful.'

'Yeah,' a male nurse said. 'And far better to bury a few staff under all the rubble if the hospital does blow up than families who might sue if their loved ones are caught up in the chaos!'

'Gee, thanks for reminding us of the buried-alive scenario,' Rachel told him. 'Just the kind of thought we need in order to keep calm!'

'You're a theatre sister—you're always calm,' the fellow told her. 'Throwing tantrums in Theatre is the surgeon's prerogative, not the nurses'.'

'Such cynicism,' Rachel murmured, but the conversation was helping everyone relax, though the mention of surgeons brought Luca back to the forefront of her mind.

Worried as she was for him, she still smiled to herself, thinking of the pleasure they'd shared, glad they'd had their time of loving. If the worst did happen then she'd have no regrets.

As long as he got out.

Survived...

'They'll have to search the hospital, floor by floor, I guess,' one of the other nurses said. 'I wouldn't like that job.'

'I don't think staff have to do it. Aren't there bomb-disposal people for things like that?'

'Whoever does it, it will take time,' Rachel said. She'd decided Luca had probably left the hospital before the alarm, and this decision filled her with an inner peace. Although every time she looked at Bobbie, dozing peacefully on the small bed, she thought what a waste it would be for the baby to have gone through such a big operation and then to lose his life because someone had a grudge against the hospital.

The minutes ticked slowly by, with announcements every now and then so they could follow the progress of the clearing of the building, and the search of each floor by members of an anti-terrorist squad.

Six hours after the original alarm had sounded, the siren wailed again, and the announcement that followed told them they were cleared to return to the wards, though the intensive care units were to wait where they were until further advice.

It was after eight that night when Rachel finally pushed Bobbie's bed out of the service elevator and back into his room, where his anxious parents were already waiting.

'I'll take over,' the nurse who was standing by told Rachel, and she walked gratefully away. An overwhelming relief was washing through her but she guessed exhaustion would be close behind.

Her feet led her automatically towards the team's rooms, knowing there'd be coffee and, with a bit of luck, some food in the refrigerator. The lights were on, and as she passed Becky's desk she realised the whole team was gathered—on chairs or perched on tables—and the expressions of their faces didn't reflect any of the relief Rachel felt.

'It's over, you guys!' she said. 'They've sounded the all clear. You should be looking happy.'

'Rachel! You're all right! I've been trying to find you.'

Luca came straight to her, put his arm around her and drew her close. She could feel his tension in the touch, and knew he'd been worried. It was nice to have someone caring about her—which thought in itself was scary.

Having someone care wasn't something she should get used to.

'I was in the ICU basement—I was with Bobbie when the alarm went off so I took him down,' she explained, feeling more tired by the minute.

But not so tired she couldn't see that her explanation had done nothing to relieve the tense atmosphere in the room.

'Something's wrong! There *was* a bomb? What don't I know?'

'The women shouldn't be part of this,' Luca declared. 'We've men enough to do the operation without them.'

Phil smiled at him.

'I feel the same way, Luca, but I'm glad I didn't say it out loud,' he said. 'Maggie would rend me limb from limb.'

'Let the women speak for themselves,' Maggie put in. 'But, first, someone should explain to Rachel what's going on.'

Alex nodded and came to stand in front of Rachel, while Luca moved just a little away.

To dissociate himself from Alex's news, or from her? By now Rachel was too stressed out to care.

'We've had a request to operate on a baby with HLHS—the same first-stage operation we performed on Bobbie Archer. But this baby is the son of a man who has political connections in a country where his politics aren't one hundred per cent popular. The people who know about these things—I'm talking anti-terrorism specialists—believe today's bomb threat was connected to the hospital's agreement to treat the baby. Somehow the parents' political enemies got wind of the arrangement, and thought a threat to the hospital might make the high-ups at Jimmie's change their minds.'

He paused and looked around as if gauging the reaction to his statement so far, then, with his eyes on Annie, he continued.

'The baby has to have the operation or, as we all know, he dies, so mind-changing isn't an option as far as I'm concerned. Annie has been in conference with the terrorism specialists and they suggested we perform the operation tonight. They feel that as soon as the night staff members are on duty, and all but ICU visitors have been cleared from the hospital, the entrances and exits to the hospital can be guarded more effectively.'

'We hope!' This from Kurt, who was looking anxiously at Rachel, no doubt seeing how tired she was, as he knew her better than the others.

'Once the operation is over, and the baby stable, he can be moved to another location. Hopefully, the people who are now in charge of that aspect of things will be more successful in keeping the location secret.'

'What gets me,' Kurt said, heading straight for the crux of the matter, 'is that if the new location's kept secret, and whoever is threatening him thinks he's still here, then the secrecy isn't much use to us. Jimmie's could still be targeted.'

Alex waved away his concerns.

'We can make it public that he's been moved. In fact, it's already been noised about that Jimmie's won't have him here at all because of the bomb scare.'

'I don't think the bomb scare is the issue,' Maggie protested. 'The baby is. You can't move him immediately post-op.'

'With life-support measures in place, we should be able to,' Alex said. 'It's a baby, Maggie. We fly them huge distances on life support in the US to bring them to specialist centres for treatment.'

'Well, I don't like it,' she said, and Rachel understood her concern. As anaesthetist, Maggie was the one who worked most closely with the baby post-operative—she and Kurt, who would be responsible for the ECMO device which could be used to provide oxygen to the baby's tissues after the operation until the surgeons were certain the repairs they had done were providing good circulation.

'Moving him is not our concern,' Alex said. 'We do the operation, and other people have to make decisions about the baby's safety.'

'I can't believe this,' Rachel said, speaking so quietly that the others who'd been arguing amiably among themselves had to stop talking to listen to her. 'We're going to operate to keep this baby alive just so some terrorist somewhere can kill him?'

The depth of emotion in her voice reminded Luca of the little he knew of this woman who had fascinated him since he'd first seen her.

She'd spent nine hours in a basement with a seriously ill baby, and now this. Was she regretting her renewed involvement with a patient?

And would that lead to regrets over her renewed involvement with men?

With him?

Alex was explaining that other babies they operated on could die in car accidents—that there were no guarantees in this world—but Luca could tell his words were falling on deaf ears where Rachel was concerned. She was pale, and he could see her knuckles gleaming whitely on her clenched fists.

Alex had moved on, throwing the meeting open to discussion, assuring everyone it was a voluntary job and if they didn't want to be part of it, no one would blame them. The team members began to talk among themselves, but no one left the room.

They would stick together and all perform their usual roles in the operation, Luca realised.

He steered Rachel towards a chair, then settled into the seat beside her, sorry he could do little more than be near her.

He took the tightly gripped hands in his and rubbed warmth into them.

'The baby might *not* be killed by terrorists. Have you thought of that? He might grow up into a fine leader, and bring peace to his country.'

She turned towards him and smiled, and what started off as a polite expression of gratitude warmed into a sheepish grin.

'Thank you!' she said, and he knew she meant it. 'My mind had got so out of kilter I'd all but lost the plot. I think I was ready to take up arms and fight for the little babe when all we have to do is get the first-stage op right so he can live to have the next one.'

She leaned forward and kissed him on the cheek, and he felt a surge of pride that she would make even that small emotional gesture in front of the others!

'Come, we will go and get you a meal in the canteen,' he said, helping her to her feet. 'We have all already eaten.'

She allowed him to help her up then smiled at him again as they left the rooms.

'You know, for an emotional Italian you're also a very practical man, Luca,' she teased. 'Always seeing to it that I'm fed!'

'It's because I love you,' he said, in much the same way he might have said because cows eat grass. 'But I said I wouldn't rush you—that I'd let you set the pace—so I don't talk of love to you, except when we're in bed.'

Rachel heard the words echo in the tired, empty cavern inside her head and tried to make sense of them.

'You love me?' Her voice was as tentative as her heartbeats, as faint as the breath fluttering in her throat.

'I do,' Luca said, pressing the button to summon the elevator.

Being practical.

Matter-of-fact!

Detached?

He didn't look at her, intent on watching the numbers light up above the door.

Rachel watched them for a while as well, but they didn't offer any help.

Luca loved her?

How could he know so soon?

She knew!

But he didn't know she loved him, so he wasn't saying it in a 'me, too' kind of way.

The elevator arrived and he guided her inside, though it felt more as if she'd stepped onto a cloud.

With every possibility she'd fall right through it and land back on earth with a bump!

'You love me?'

She heard her own voice repeat the question, saw the other occupants of the metal conveyance turn to stare at her, and registered both Luca's deep chuckle and the warmth of his hands as he pressed one of hers between them.

'I do, though I probably wouldn't have shared it with the whole world just yet.'

'It's not the whole world,' Rachel told him, 'only...' she stopped to count '...five people.'

The elevator reached the ground floor and the five grinning passengers disembarked, all offering their good wishes, and luck, one woman adding, 'I'd stop arguing if I were you, and snaffle him up.'

She would if she could just get her head around it.

'It's a funny time to tell me.'

Luca made a grab for the closing door and it slid open again. He guided her out, then turned so he was looking at her, still holding one of her hands in both of his.

'When the siren went off, I didn't know where you were. There was a bomb scare. I thought of something happening to you. Of you dying! It was as if I'd died. Then the agony of you dying without knowing how I felt about you—I had to tell you.'

'Agony for you?'

'Agony for me,' he said softly, then he leaned forward and kissed her on the lips before reverting to the practical Italian once again and leading her towards the canteen.

CHAPTER NINE

'I WILL not have men with guns in my theatre!'

'We are the baby's bodyguards—we go everywhere with him.'

'Not into my theatre!' Alex sounded adamant—and not a little angry.

It was two hours later. Rachel had eaten. Well, she remembered putting food into her mouth, though for a million dollars couldn't have said what it was.

Mostly, she'd tried to think. Looking at Luca and trying to think and then, when that didn't help clear the confusion in her head, not looking at Luca and trying to think.

'Do not fret about it,' he had said at one stage. 'I would not have spoken if I'd known you'd be so surprised. I thought you must have known, but now you're worrying and that won't do. I do not ask that you love me back, only that you accept how I feel. So, relax and let your mind focus now on the operation.'

They'd parted in the lounge, she to change and check the theatre, he to go into conference with Phil and Alex. So now she was waiting in the theatre for the patient to be wheeled in, listening to a conversation nearly as bizarre as the one she'd had with Luca earlier.

She'd turned at the sound of Alex's voice and now realised the baby was here, though whether he'd come further than the door depended on whether Alex won the argument he was currently having with two burly men.

Through the open doorway she could hear a woman crying softly, and men's voices conversing in a language she didn't understand. Annie's voice as well, explaining, placating, trying desperately to sort out the situation.

Then Alex's voice again.

'I don't care if they wait on Mars, but they're not coming into my theatre.'

Luca came in from the changing rooms, crossing the theatre towards Rachel, the anxiety and concern in his eyes warming her.

'You are all right?'

As ever, when he was stressed, his English became more formal.

'I'm fine,' she assured him. Utter lie! 'Don't worry about me, worry about that baby.'

She nodded towards the double doors that led from the passage to the theatre.

'There's more trouble?' Luca's voice expressed his disbelief.

'Only men with guns,' Kurt told him. 'Strange as it might sound, Alex doesn't want them in Theatre.'

'I should think not,' Luca said, moving closer to Rachel. 'This is a ridiculous situation, particularly with women involved.'

'Hey, Luca, enough of this protectiveness where Rachel and I are concerned,' Maggie, who'd followed him into theatre, told him. 'Women fought long and hard for equal rights—and now we've got them, we have to take equal responsibility.'

'I still don't like it,' Luca said stubbornly, and

Rachel smiled at his insistence. It was old-fashioned but nice, that kind of chivalry.

And he loved her?

Now movement at the door suggested Alex had prevailed, as he and Phil walked beside the trolley bearing the baby boy.

Rachel studied the face of the man with whom she'd worked for so long. It was set and hard, his eyes grim, and she wondered if he was having second thoughts about operating.

'Luca, would you and Scott open while Phil and I scrub? Maggie, you set to go? Kurt, Rachel, you two ready?'

He barely stayed for their nods before crossing to the scrub room, where a nurse waited with gowns and gloves for both surgeons. Maggie hooked the baby to her monitors, Ned set up a metal frame over the baby's head so it was protected during the operation, and Rachel spread drapes across his little body.

'I wonder why the incidence of congenital heart defects is higher in boys than girls—with nearly all the different defects, we seem to see more boys than girls,' Kurt said, making conversation while checking that the plastic tubes that would run from the baby to his machine and back again to the infant were all out of the way of the operating staff.

Rachel knew one kinked tube could mean death for an infant and, though nobody was saying anything, she was pretty sure they all felt the threat of the men with guns outside the theatre doors.

'The men with guns, who apparently are the baby's personal bodyguards, have been replaced by hospital security men—also with guns,' Alex explained when he returned, ready to take over the lead role from

Luca. 'They will wait in the corridor outside Theatre while the other bodyguards—and there are four in all, two for the father as well—will wait with the family somewhere up on the admin floor.'

'Does that mean that if the baby happens to not live through this operation, we won't be gunned down in Theatre?' Kurt's plaintive question made everyone smile and released some of the tension the men-with-guns scenario had built up.

'No, they'll wait and gun us down in the street,' Ned said, but Rachel had spent more than enough emotion for one day and didn't find it a joking matter.

'This baby will not die,' she said fiercely. 'Not if you all concentrate on your jobs, instead of thinking about what's happening outside.'

'Hear, hear,' Alex said, carefully cutting a small patch from the baby's pericardium and setting it in a liquid solution in case he needed it later. 'This baby is no different to all the others we have operated on. We will do our best for him—no one can ask more than that.'

But it seemed fate could, for the baby fibrillated badly when he went onto the bypass machine, and had to be resuscitated on the table.

Alex gave sharp orders and Maggie fed different drugs into the drip line—drugs to prevent fibrillation and to restore the balance of chemicals in the baby's blood. Anxious moments passed, Rachel's gaze going from the baby to the monitors and back again.

'Should we shock?' This from Phil, while behind him Ned stood by with the generator and paddles ready should they be needed.

'No, he's stable again,' Maggie said, but the tension in the room had tightened considerably, so it

seemed to Rachel the air had become solid and now
vibrated with the slightest move.

Alex worked swiftly and, though his fingers
seemed too big and clumsy to fit within the baby's
small chest cavity, he cut and stitched with delicate
efficiency.

'His blood's thickening,' Kurt warned, and Alex
ordered more drugs from Maggie to thin the blood so
it would pass more easily through the machine. Too
thick and it could clot, too thin and the slightest mistake could lead to a bad haemorrhage—it was a razor-
sharp line they walked as the surgeons worked, re-
aligning blood vessels and opening valves in an
attempt to give the little one a chance of life.

'OK, three minutes and we'll be off bypass,' Alex
announced. 'I'll give the word, Kurt.'

But no one breathed easy until the pump stopped
and they saw the little ill-formed heart beat valiantly.

Alex stayed and closed, as if this baby were more
important than others, but Rachel guessed he couldn't
walk away from his team and chose to close rather
than make it obvious he was hanging around in case
of trouble.

He closed each layer with fastidious care, first the
pericardium, then the chest, looping one curved needle into the bone on one side, then the needle on the
other end of the thin wire into the other side, positioning four wires before he and Phil, using plier-like
needle-holders, crossed them over and knotted them
tight, then clipped off the ends and pressed them flat
so they wouldn't cause problems to the baby later.

Finally the skin was closed, and the wound dressed.
They were done!

'Maggie's right,' Alex said, when he finally

stepped back from the table and unplugged his head-light, rubbing wearily at the indentations it had left on his forehead. 'We can't transfer him immediately. We've all we need to keep him stable right here in Theatre. What say we keep him here until morning, see how he's doing, then make a decision?'

That way, Rachel realised, the men with guns wouldn't scare the living daylights out of all the parents sitting by their children in the PICU, and they were not endangering anyone else's life.

'I am happy to stay,' Luca said, 'but surely most of the staff should leave.'

'He's my responsibility post-op so I'd be staying anyway,' Maggie said. 'I might as well watch over him here in Theatre as anywhere else.'

'Well, if you lot are in, so am I,' Rachel told them, 'though I might do a bit of my waiting in the lounge. Shall we take turns to have a break in there?'

'Good idea,' Phil replied. 'Alex, you and I will go first. We'll take a break, grab some coffee and a bite to eat and be back in about an hour.'

Alex didn't argue, and Rachel, who knew how fiercely he concentrated during an operation, thought tiredness had probably prompted him to accompany Phil so meekly out of the door. But Maggie had a different idea.

'They're plotting something, those two,' she said, looking questioningly at Luca. 'Are you in on it?'

Luca spread his hands wide.

'Me? We've all been here, gathered around the table, concentrating on the baby—what chance has anyone had to plot?'

'Well, I know Phil, and he's plotting,' Maggie announced.

'Alex will want to see the family,' Scott suggested. 'He always does straight after an op.'

'Maybe he'll call Annie from the lounge and have her do it,' Ned suggested, and Rachel realised they were all feeling residual tension, for the whys and wherefores of the two men's departure to be so closely analysed.

The theatre phone rang an hour later, and Ned answered it, spoke for a while, then hung up.

'That was Alex, apologising for keeping us in the dark, but apparently Phil had a brilliant idea and they had to run it past the parents—using Annie as a go-between.'

'So tell us!' Maggie demanded, but at that moment the inner door opened and Alex ushered in two people, a man and a woman, both so obviously distressed Rachel knew they were the parents.

Phil, like Alex, still in theatre scrubs, followed behind them.

'Let them be with the little boy for a few moments,' Alex said, and the team members, with the exception of Maggie at the monitor, all fell back. The pair spoke quietly, their eyes feasting on their child, then the man put his arm around the woman's shoulders and she lifted a handkerchief to her eyes. Alex joined them and all three walked out into the corridor. Phil waited until the doors closed behind them, before explaining.

'They had to agree to our idea, and then to see the baby, but we are giving out that he died during the operation. I thought of it when he fibrillated—thought it might be an answer to how to keep him safe post-op. As far as the world—and that includes everyone in the hospital who is not in this room—is concerned, what you saw was the parents' last farewell to their son. The baby died in Theatre. Annie is organising all the things that have to be done, including a memory box, and while some of you might feel this is tempting fate, it's the only way we could see of keeping the baby here, yet removing any risk to the hospital and staff.'

He paused, then looked at each of them in turn.

'To ask you to swear you won't betray this child would be melodramatic, but you must all know in your hearts how important it is to maintain the charade. We've had a devil of a job convincing the baby's bodyguards that they must also leave with the coffin that will be arranged, or the plan won't work, but having got them out of the way, then it would be really bad if someone on the team gave the game away.'

Luca watched the team members all nod, and wondered at the unity Alex had achieved among his staff—though some of them had not been with him for long. Would he be able to bring such a team together when his clinic opened?

And would that team include Rachel?

Dared he ask her?

What of her loyalty to Alex?

Luca found that he, who usually planned his life so carefully, finding answers to all his problems through thought and application, had no idea of the answers to these questions. Things had seemed to be going well until his fear for her earlier today had prompted him to mention his love.

Since then it was as if she'd departed to some other place, where words alone were not enough to reach her. Tonight, or tomorrow—whenever they could be alone—he would show her as well as tell her of his love.

He would also tell her of his plan for them to be a team in every way, building up the clinic together, sharing the future.

'Well, I for one am desperate for coffee,' Kurt announced. 'Seeing a dead baby breathe does it to me all the time.'

And that was something else, Luca thought, watching Kurt hook his arm around Rachel and guide her out of the room. Would his team joke and fool around to relieve tension in the theatre? This was something he hadn't come across before. Leaving the circulating nurse, Ned, Maggie and Phil in Theatre with the baby, Luca followed Kurt and Rachel to the lounge where Kurt was already pouring coffee.

'One for you, Luca?' Kurt asked, waving the coffee-pot in the air.

'Please,' Luca said, then he sat down beside Rachel and took her hand.

'You're all right?'

She turned towards him with a tired smile and he noticed the lines of weariness on her face and the dark shadows beneath her eyes. Guilt that he might be responsible for some of her tiredness struck him, but he didn't think an apology would work. Not here and now, anyway.

'It shouldn't be long before the baby can be moved somewhere else,' he said, hoping to contribute to the lightening of tension, 'and we can all go home.'

'It's not the staying here that bothers me,' Rachel told him, accepting the cup of coffee from Kurt with such a sweet smile Luca wished it had been for him.

'It's the state of our world when a tiny baby needs two bodyguards.'

'But kids all over the world, from wealthy, or famous or in some way important families, have bodyguards, Rach,' Kurt reminded her. 'Having fame or money isn't all it's cracked up to be—it makes people very vulnerable.'

'Well, I wouldn't like my kids—if I had them—to have to spend their lives shadowed by men with guns, so maybe it's a good thing I'm not wealthy or famous or even a little bit important.'

Rachel turned to Luca.

'You grew up with money. Did it bother you?'

She saw his face close as she asked the question and immediately regretted it, but it was too late to take it back.

'How can you be so innocent, so trusting?' he demanded. 'Lots of terrible things happen all over the world, they always have done and will continue to do so, yet you still believe the world is a safe and wonderful place.'

'But it is, by and large,' Rachel argued. 'I know bad things happen to good people but on the whole there's a lot more positives than negatives happening. Look at the development in cancer cures, particularly the results for childhood cancer.'

'And take our own field,' Kurt put in. 'Not so long ago, babies with HLHS were cared for until they died, but now we can fix them to the extent they can lead near-normal lives.'

Luca smiled at him.

'Yes, here is plenty to be optimistic about. Maybe the pessimism I sometimes feel is to do with my own personal experience.'

'Well, I brought up the gloomy subject,' Rachel admitted, 'talking about bodyguards, and guns. Maybe we can agree to disagree.'

But although she spoke lightly, she was aware that she'd lost the closeness she'd felt with Luca earlier. Her personal question had struck some kind of nerve, and erected a barrier between them.

Perhaps that was just as well. In spite of the wondrous nature of the time they'd spent together, and the joy they'd shared in their love-making, she was still uncertain about their affair and afraid, for all Luca's words of love, that it was doomed to be just that—an affair.

Rachel stayed on in the lounge, but Luca had departed soon after the strained conversation with her and Kurt about the state of the world.

Kurt, too, had wandered off, so she was on her own. And although she was physically tired, her mind buzzed with speculation about what lay ahead—for the baby, and his parents, for herself and Luca…

No, better not to think about herself and Luca! He'd talked of love, but had he meant it?

And even if he had, what did it mean?

Her tired mind couldn't decide, but neither could she stop it going around in circles, getting nowhere.

Remembering she'd shoved her theatre nurses' newsletter into her handbag some days ago but still hadn't read it, she went to her locker and found her bag, pulling the magazine from its depths.

Back in the lounge, she flicked through it, wondering if there were any articles to hold her interest in her current state of near-exhaustion.

Nothing caught her eye, though on her second pass through it she saw the ad.

Or the photo of the man in the centre of the ad.

Luca!

Exhaustion forgotten, she spread the flimsy newsletter out and stared at the double-page spread. A photo of a sparkling new building took up a quarter of the page opposite the photo, and below it were lists of staff positions that needed to be filled. The ad had been placed by an agency in the US that Rachel knew by name, mainly because it was so big it recruited staff to work in jobs all over the world.

Some positions had been filled, but the largest and seemingly most urgent advertisement sprang out of the page at her.

Physician's assistant—twelve-month renegotiable contracts—the pay range enough to make her eyes widen in disbelief. Luca was offering serious money for someone to assist him in Theatre.

Language would be no barrier, the ad assured would-be candidates. Lessons in Italian would be provided for all foreign staff.

Reading through the qualifications and experience required, Rachel knew the job description could have been structured just for her, but with this knowledge came suspicion.

She tried to banish it with common sense. The magazine was a month old or even older, and the position had probably been filled.

But what if it hadn't?

One way to find out! Newsletter in hand, she headed for the phone, trying to work out the time difference in her head. It would be morning in

California where the agency had its head office. A quick phone call—that's all it would take.

'I'm sorry,' a female voice told her, after she'd been switched from one person to another for what seemed an interminable time, 'but the advertiser has recently advised us he has someone in mind for a PA. But we're involved with another surgeon putting a paediatric cardiac team together for a hospital down in Australia. St James's Children's Hospital in a city called Sydney. Starting date in about three months' time. Would you like to work there?'

Without bothering to explain she was already working in that exact location but in the trial unit, Rachel hung up.

So the advertiser for the clinic in Italy had someone in mind, did he?

Someone called Rachel Lerini?

Had Luca been wooing her, not because he loved her, as he'd so recently professed, but because he needed a PA for his new clinic?

Was that why he'd once asked her about working after marriage?

Although maybe marriage wouldn't come into it!

Maybe he thought good times in bed and the mention of love would be enough to entice her away from Alex.

Could this really be happening? How could she have given in to attraction against all her better judgement, then—worst of all—fallen in love with the man, and not realised he was using her?

What was she? Stupid?

Damn it all—the signs were all there. He'd *told* her Italians were practical! But when he'd questioned her on her feelings about having more children, and combining a family and work, she'd thought he was being understanding and empathetic, concerned only for *her*!

What a fool she'd been.

Pain she'd sworn she'd never feel again seared through her. The pain of loss, grief, betrayal…

She folded the newsletter and shoved it back into the depths of her handbag.

'You mustn't frown like that. You are right. The world, on the whole, is a good place. And if we do not keep believing that, and accepting adjustments to our way of life so we can continue to live in freedom, then the bad guys win!'

Luca had returned, unnoticed by her while she was fuming—angry at herself for being conned by a handsome man with a smooth tongue and enticing accent.

Angry at the pain!

So angry she barely heard the words he'd said—barely remembered the conversation that had prompted them.

He sat beside her, but when he put his arm around her shoulders she moved away, her body rigid with distress. Unable to find the words she needed to accuse him of betrayal, she reached down and pulled the newsletter out of her bag, smoothing out the page before shoving it in front of him.

'Your ad?'

He looked at the ad, then at her, studying her intently, as if trying to read her thoughts.

'My picture is there—you must know it is an advertisement for my clinic,' he said quietly, but quietness did nothing to soothe her increasing agitation.

'And is the PA's position filled?' The ice forming

again inside her made the words cold, and as clear and sharp as scalpels.

Not that she'd draw blood. He was heartless. Bloodless! He *had* to be!

'I do not know,' he said slowly. 'I had hoped...' he added, then stopped, confirming Rachel's worst fears.

Ice gave way to molten rage.

'Hoped I might fit the bill? Is that why you made such a play for me? To get a PA for your precious clinic? Is that why you paid me ridiculous compliments, chased after me, even went so far as to say you loved me? Is that what it's all been about?'

He looked at her, sorrow in his dark eyes, and the love she felt for him pierced her anger, weakening her to the extent she was silently begging him to deny it.

Just one word—that's all she needed.

One small, gently spoken, slightly accented 'No'.

She held her breath then let it out in a great whoosh of despair when he said, not no, or even words that meant it.

'I cannot honestly say it never crossed my mind,' he told her. 'But my feelings for you—they're for you the person, not you the PA. That's the truth.'

She stared at him, unable to believe he wasn't protesting more. He should be trying to convince her of his love. Assuring her of it—kissing her even!

'Truth! It's just a word to you,' she snapped. 'Like trust! I *did* trust you, Luca, and look what happened. It's like the clothes you had sent to your apartment without consulting me. You think money buys everything—that whatever you want you can have, and whatever is best for you must be right for anyone else involved. You could have told me about the job, asked me if I'd be interested, but, no, you have the hide to phone the agency—when? The day after we spent the night in bed? That soon?—and you tell them the position is filled. So sure of yourself—of your charm and looks and money—it never occurred to you I might not want your stupid job, or that I might just be having an affair with you for the sake of it.'

She paused, drew a deep breath, then added one huge lie, 'And I was! It was therapeutic—nothing more. To get over my non-involvement with men. So there!'

The 'so there' was definitely childish but she was so upset it had just popped out.

Luca stared at her.

'Rachel—' he began, then Alex walked in.

'Luca?'

'One moment, Alex, and I will be with you.'

Rachel looked from Luca to Alex, then back to Luca, feeling tension that had nothing to do with her own distress vibrating through the air between the three of them.

She waited for Luca to finish what he'd been about to say, but all he did was look at her with sorrow in his eyes, then he took her hand, lifted it to his lips, and pressed a kiss on it.

'I must go now,' he said, and she had the strangest feeling he was saying goodbye, not just for now but for ever.

And in spite of betrayal and pain and rage, she felt her heart break as surely as it had broken when Reece had died.

Numb with despair, she watched him stand up, cross the room to where Alex waited then, with a final

glance in her direction, he followed Alex out of
the door.

Out of her life?

Why would she think that?

But, given what had happened, why should she
care?

CHAPTER TEN

AT FOUR-THIRTY that morning, two long black cars with tinted windows drew up outside the hospital's staff entrance and a sombre procession led by two burly bodyguards, one carrying a small coffin, trailed from the building to the cars. Two more men assisted a woman who was obviously near collapse, while Alex walked with his arm around a man's shoulders, talking quietly.

He saw them into the cars, watched them drive away, then went back inside the building, past security men who nodded respectfully at him.

At eight a.m. an ambulance, which had come through the city traffic with its siren shrieking, screamed into the emergency bay at A and E and unloaded a blood-spattered patient. Doctors and nurses ran beside the gurney as it was pushed into A and E and the ambulance drew away, waiting in a parking bay until the attendant who'd accompanied the patient completed his paperwork and returned.

The ambulance driver hated waiting in this particular parking area as it was close to the service exit and laundry trucks were always pulling up there. Service staff milled around, bringing great bundles of laundry out to load into the truck, while other trucks brought fresh linen back, delivering it to the same door, causing traffic chaos because there were never enough parking spaces.

But the chaos helped disguise the fact that a very

small baby had been loaded, wrapped like laundry, into the ambulance, and the specialist staff waiting in the back of the vehicle had already hooked him up to monitors and machines that had been put in place earlier at another hospital.

The driver and his partner knew nothing more than that the baby had been the victim of an attempted kidnapping and was being moved in secrecy to another hospital.

Interstate, presumably, as the ambo driver had orders to take his passengers directly to the airport.

At seven-thirty, as weary staff left the hospital at the end of their night shift, the members of Alex's surgical team who were still in the hospital mingled with those departing and headed for home. Rachel was grateful for the support of Kurt's arm around her waist. She was so tense with tiredness she felt a loud noise might split her open, but the tiredness was a boon, for it stopped her thinking about Luca—and about love and betrayal and pain and loss.

Almost stopped her thinking!

She heard a groan escape from her lips and felt Kurt's arm tighten around her waist.

'He'll be quite safe, you know,' Kurt said, and it took a few minutes for the words to sink in.

'What do you mean, he'll be quite safe? Who do you mean?'

She'd stopped walking and Kurt turned to look at her.

'Luca, of course.'

She watched horror dawn on Kurt's face.

'You don't know?'

He sounded upset, and hesitated, as if uncertain what to tell her.

'Well?' she demanded.

'Luca went with the baby. I thought you knew. I was sure he'd have told you.'

'He went where with the baby? I fell asleep, remember, and next thing I know the baby had gone.'

'Back to his own country—the baby's country, not Luca's. He went as medical support. Maggie, Phil, Alex, they all wanted to go, but Luca pointed out it would be suspicious if any of the team suddenly disappeared for a few days, while he was not a team member and would not be missed by anyone, even hospital staff, who would assume he had completed his time with Alex and returned home.'

'And will he return home when he can leave the baby?'

Anguish that she might never see him again—and guilt that they'd parted as they had—bit into her.

Kurt held his arms wide.

'I don't know, Rach. I assumed he'd be back but no one actually said anything. I mean, he left with the baby—he didn't go home and pack or anything.'

'He has a manager at his apartments who can rustle up food and clothing at the drop of a hat—no doubt he'll do it for him anyway,' Rachel said, adding bitterness to all the other hurt inside her. Even in her exhausted state, she could feel her heart icing over.

Luca *had* been saying goodbye.

'Did you see the news this morning?'

Maggie asked the question as Kurt and Rachel walked into the rooms the following morning.

'What news?'

'Early morning news on TV—they had film of fighting in the streets. Apparently the government in the baby's country—you know what baby—has been overthrown, and the army is now in control.'

Fear that was colder than the ice around her heart gripped Rachel and though she opened her mouth to ask questions, it was Kurt who spoke.

'Was the baby's family with the old government? Do we know that for sure? Maybe the father was connected to the army who are now in control.'

Maggie shrugged.

'Phil understood they were part of the old governing body,' she said, 'but you'd think if they were, they'd have had advance warning of a coup and not returned there.'

'They would need a hospital for the baby,' Rachel said. 'Where else could they have gone?'

'With Luca on board the plane, maybe they went to Italy. He could have arranged for the baby to be admitted somewhere there.'

But within a day the team learned the plane had landed as scheduled, the family apparently unaware of the new turmoil in their country.

'They landed and walked right into the hands of the people they'd been trying to avoid,' Kurt said, as he and Rachel watched the news bulletin that evening. 'What a waste all our deception was if the rebels got the baby anyway!'

'There's no mention of Luca or the baby—just that the family have been imprisoned along with the rest of the previous government,' Rachel told him, furiously flicking through channels on the television in the hope another news broadcast might tell her more.

'He's a foreigner on a humanitarian mission—they won't hurt him,' Kurt said, but Rachel found no comfort in the lie. Kurt knew as well as she did that members of humanitarian missions were considered fair game in war-torn countries. 'And surely they wouldn't have hurt the baby.'

'Ho!' she said. 'As if! We're talking about the people who threatened to bomb our entire hospital in order to kill the baby.'

'Maybe not,' Kurt argued. 'As far as we know, all they really wanted was to stop us treating him. I would say that the worst scenario is that Luca's at the hospital with the baby, and under a kind of house arrest—hospital arrest.'

Kurt was trying to cheer her up, but memories of the way she'd parted from Luca haunted Rachel, and regret for the way she'd spoken—the accusations she'd made—made her heart hurt.

Needing something of him near her, she found the newsletter that had prompted her anger, searching through it for the ad—for his photo.

She ran her fingers across the beloved face, trying to will him safe. She felt helpless, and frustrated by her helplessness.

'Have you read the article?' Kurt asked, coming to sit beside her and looking across at the magazine.

Rachel shook her head.

'I read the ad and that was it,' she said, looking at the words beneath the photo but unable to focus because of the fear she felt for him.

'Then give it here. I'll read it.'

'Reading a stupid article won't help rescue him,' she snapped, not because she was angry with Kurt but because she didn't want to pass over the photo.

Which was dead-set pathetic!

Kurt refused to be put off, easing it from her fingers

and bending his head to read the article that accompanied the photo.

'Forty-bed clinic specialising in cardiac surgery. Apparently his sister is also a cardiac surgeon, but treats adult patients. They'll both work there.'

'He's got four sisters,' Rachel said, pulling the stray memory from some recess in her mind.

But Kurt was no longer listening and something in the way he sat drew her attention.

His eyes raced across the page, and every now and then he muttered, 'Oh, no!' but it wasn't until Rachel tried to snatch the newsletter away that he shared what he'd learned.

'Luca was kidnapped as a child! Remember that funny conversation we had in the lounge—about living with bodyguards? Well, apparently, when he was five he was kidnapped and held for two weeks.'

'And now he's being held prisoner again,' Rachel whispered, horror weakening her bones. 'Think of the memories it will bring back. Poor Luca!'

Her hands twisted in her lap, desperate for occupation, and in the end she knew she couldn't sit around doing nothing.

'I'm going to Italy,' she announced. 'I'll find his family—find out what they're doing, whether they've had contact with him.'

She looked beseechingly at Kurt.

'Would that be OK, do you think?'

'I think it would be a great idea,' he said gently, 'but you don't speak the language, Rach. For all you know, Cavaletti might be like Smith or Brown in Italy. How will you find the family?'

'I'll take the magazine and point. There's a photo of the new clinic. I'll show it to people until someone tells me how to get there—and once I've got that far, surely I can find the sister who's a doctor.'

Kurt shook his head, but whether in disbelief or disapproval she couldn't tell, neither did she care. She got up and crossed to the phone, dialling Alex's number, reminding him, when he answered, that she was due holidays.

'You're not going to do anything stupid?' Alex asked, and she realised everyone in the team must know about her and Luca. Remembering a conversation they'd had on this subject, she found she didn't mind one bit.

'I'm going to Italy,' she said. 'I can't sit here not knowing what's happening. Ned's good enough at his work to take my place.'

'You go with my blessing—our blessing, because Annie's here by my side. You phone the airlines and I'll see if I can get in touch with someone at Luca's practice—it will be morning over there. Call me back when you have a flight number and arrival time.'

Rachel let the phone drop back into its cradle, tears she couldn't control sliding down her cheeks.

'Damn it all! Alex gave you bad news over the phone!'

Kurt was beside her, hugging her, patting her back and smoothing her hair in comfort.

Rachel couldn't speak but shook her head and let the tears dampen his shirt. Then the storm passed and she raised her head.

'It wasn't bad news,' she said, smiling weakly at her comforter. 'But Alex was so kind and understanding and helpful, it was too much for me, and suddenly I was crying.'

She sniffed back the last remnants of tears and offered him another watery smile.

'I'm better now. I have to phone the airlines.'

'I'll do that,' Kurt offered. 'You get yourself a cup of coffee and sit down.'

Two hours later she was booked on a flight that left Sydney early the following morning for Rome with a connecting flight to Milan.

'Someone will meet you in Milan,' Alex, who'd insisted on driving her to the airport, told her as he followed her as far as the security check. Then he took her hand and said, 'Good luck, Rachel. You know all our love and best wishes are with you. If ever a woman deserved a happy ending, it's you.'

He kissed her on the cheek, and with tears again coursing down her cheeks she walked through the metal detector and waited for her hand-luggage to be scanned.

Security checks!

Luca had been right—if they didn't accept the adjustments they had to make, and get on with their lives, then the 'bad guys', as he'd called them, would win. In the world of medicine, there was no differentiating between the good guys and the bad guys— if people needed care they should get it. And in so many instances there were no good or bad guys, just people with different beliefs.

Thinking philosophy was better than thinking of Luca in danger, so she pondered the problems of the world as she boarded the plane, then ate her meal and settled herself to sleep her way across half the world.

At Rome airport, she went through customs and more security checks before boarding a local plane for Milan. Somehow, in the ten hours between making her booking and leaving the flat, Kurt had managed to get hold of an Italian phrase book for her though, looking at it now, she doubted it would be much use to her.

She didn't think she'd need a phrase for 'Where can I buy shoes?'

But she flicked through the phrase book anyway, remembering words Luca had whispered to her, and learning they were, as she'd suspected, words of love.

His voice, husky with desire, echoed in her head and she felt a little of her hard-won control slipping. But falling apart wasn't going to help Luca. She had to find his family and plan what *would* help him.

Milan airport was even more crowded than Rome, although she'd only been in transit in Rome so probably hadn't seen all of it. But walking off the plane into a sea of excited Italians, all calling and gesticulating to friends and relations, made her realise just how alone she was.

Until someone grabbed her arm and a small woman with grey streaks in her severely pulled-back dark hair said, 'You are Rachel?'

Rachel looked at the stranger and nodded.

'Ha, I knew!' the woman said, turning away to beckon to someone in the crowd. 'Beautiful hair, Luca said, so I knew at once, though Sylvana and Paola did not believe.'

Two more women, younger, joined them, both smiling and both looking so like Luca Rachel had to bite her lip to stop from crying yet again.

'I am Paola,' the taller of the two said, then she introduced her sister and her mother. 'Our two other sisters and their husbands are all talking to the diplomatic people. My husband is trying to find out things from a newspaper magnate he knows.'

Rachel tried to absorb this information but all she could think of was the kindness of these people, and how they seemed to consider her as family, wrapping her in the security that came with belonging.

Had Luca told them more than the colour of her hair?

'We will go to my place, which is near the clinic,' Paola said. 'I'm the other surgeon in the family. We have good friends at home by the telephone, and at Luca's office at the hospital, so if any news comes, we will hear it as soon as possible.'

Rachel allowed herself to be led away, first to the baggage retrieval area, then out of the airport to where a long black limousine waited at the kerb. A chauffeur leapt from the driving seat to take her case and open doors, and they all clambered in, Mrs Cavaletti sitting next to Rachel and holding tightly to her hand.

And suddenly Rachel felt what the older woman must be going through—the risk of losing a beloved only son, and not for the first time.

'How do you stand it?' she asked, and Luca's mother smiled at her.

'With a whole lot of faith,' Mrs Cavaletti said. 'Faith in Luca for a start—he is strong and he has so much work left to do in his life he will not give up easily. And faith that things will come out right in the end.'

She gave a little nod, and squeezed Rachel's hand. 'That is the strongest belief. We must never for a moment think it won't come out right.'

'Mamma is big on positive thoughts,' Sylvana, who was on the jump-seat opposite the other three, said, and Rachel was struck by the strong American accent in the English words.

'Have you lived in America?' she asked the younger sister, and Sylvana rushed to explain how a year as an exchange student had led to her continuing to do a university degree over there.

'Sylvana is engaged to a young doctor in New York,' Paola explained, then she smiled at Rachel. 'We have been saying we shall lose one sister to America, but that country, from what Luca has told us, will be giving one back to us.'

Rachel's heartbeat speeded up. She remembered Luca saying his family talked about everything—and laughed, cried, hugged and generally shared. But for him to have spoken so much of her? Maybe his love was genuine.

Or maybe he'd just been assuring Paola he had a good PA for the clinic...

'No negative thoughts,' Sylvana murmured, and Rachel realised she must be frowning. But Sylvana was right—the first priority was to get Luca home safe, and after that...surely they'd have a chance to talk, to sort out things like love and trust...

Paola's apartment was in a tall, glass-fronted building, the inside decorated in white and black and grey, sleekly modern and quite stunning though, having driven past some really beautiful old stone buildings, Rachel was a little disappointed not to be seeing the inside of one of them.

'Luca's apartment is in an older building,' Mrs Cavaletti said, and Rachel turned to the woman in surprise.

'I sometimes thought Luca could read my mind,

but I didn't know it was a family trait,' she said, and Mrs Cavaletti smiled.

'Your face tells all—it is so expressive it is no wonder my son could read it.'

'That can't be true,' Rachel protested, thinking how she'd never told Luca of her love, but wondering just how often it might have been written on her face.

'It is,' Sylvana told her. 'I'm not as good as Mamma and Luca at reading faces, but even I could see it.'

Paola, who had disappeared when they entered the apartment, returned with a tray holding a coffee-pot and cups.

'No news, but I'll call my husband shortly and see if he has made any progress.'

By late afternoon Rachel knew one more cup of coffee would have her hanging from the ceiling, and if she didn't get out in the fresh air, she'd fall asleep in the chair.

'I think jet-lag is catching up with me,' she said. 'Would you mind if I went out for a walk?'

'I'll come with you,' Sylvana offered, then she laughed. 'I can see you want to be alone, so I won't talk to you, just make sure you don't get lost.'

Rachel thanked her, but found she didn't mind Sylvana talking, especially as the younger woman prattled on almost ceaselessly about her fiancé in New York and the wedding that was planned for January.

They returned an hour later, Rachel feeling revived, though she didn't remember many of the details of dress, flowers or wedding cake. Three men had joined the waiting women, and Paola introduced Rachel to her husband, a colleague of his and another man who was from some government department.

'The government has word of Luca,' Mrs Cavaletti said quietly, her dark eyes sombre as she looked at Rachel. 'It appears he was offered safe passage out of the country, because the people now in command have no bad feelings against our country, but the hospital is largely unstaffed and what staff remains is over-worked, treating wounded from the fighting, so Luca has elected to remain, in part to care for the baby but also to help out in other ways.'

Rachel felt her knees give way, then someone grabbed her shoulders and led her to a chair, where she sank down and rested her head in her hands.

'Stupid, stupid man!' she muttered, oblivious to the stupid man's family gathered around her. 'Why would he do that? Why not leave and come home? The baby is going to need another operation in a few months, and if there's no one there who can perform it he'll die anyway. But, no, Luca has to stay and care for him.'

She shook her head, the last of the anger leaching out of her, then she looked up at the people watching her in various degrees of amazement and distress.

'I'm sorry—of course he'd have chosen to stay. Being Luca, he couldn't have done anything else, but it's all so senseless, isn't it? First the baby's parents risk their lives to get him to Australia for the operation, and probably put their government at risk because the coup happened while they were gone, and now this—a situation that's lose-lose whichever way you look at it.'

'But it may not be,' Sylvana said. 'When things settle down, the hospital in that place will find new doctors and maybe one will be a surgeon who can do the next operation on the baby.'

Rachel had to smile.

'I remember Luca saying something like that to me on a day when I was thinking negative thoughts. Thanks for that, Sylvana!' Rachel turned to Mrs Cavaletti. 'And that's the last negative thought from me,' she promised.

She looked up at the government official.

'If you have learned this from someone in the country, is there two-way communication? Can you speak to people over there?'

The man looked dubious, but perhaps because he didn't understand her, for one of the other men translated.

'We are talking to them, yes,' he said to Rachel.

'Then maybe you can offer them help. Tell them you have heard the hospital is understaffed and you know a nurse who is willing to go over there.'

'You can't do that!' Sylvana shrieked, while Paola added her own protest, but Mrs Cavaletti seemed to understand, for she took Rachel's hand again and held it very tightly.

'I can and will go if it's at all possible,' Rachel said to Luca's sisters, then had to explain. 'You see, for a long time I've been...well, uninvolved is the only way I can explain it. Detached from life—living but not living. Luca reminded me just how rich life can be, but it is he who has made it that way. Without him, well, I think it would lose all its flavour again, so I might just as well be with him over there as dying slowly inside without him here in Italy—or anywhere else for that matter.'

She looked directly at his mother.

'You understand?'

The woman nodded, then she took Rachel's face in

her hands and kissed her first on one cheek, then on the other.

'You will go with my blessing.'

At ten that night, when Rachel had been dozing in a chair while Luca's family members and friends had come and gone around her, the man from the government returned.

'We have found a doctor who is joining a Red Cross mission due to leave from Switzerland in the morning. He will collect you in an hour. You will drive to Zurich, then fly part of the way and finish the journey by truck. The Red Cross people have cleared you to go with the mission.'

Rachel couldn't believe it had all been so easy— or seemingly easy. She shook herself awake and stood up, looking around for her luggage. She'd take only necessities—change of panties and toiletries, a spare pair of jeans and a couple of T-shirts, water—in her small backpack.

Paola was ushering her towards the bathroom.

'It might be the last running water you see for a while,' she joked, and Rachel realised the whole family was thinking of her.

But excitement soon gave way to tiredness and she slept as they drove through the night, missing the views of the wondrous mountains she knew must be outside the window of the car, too tired to even register a trip through a foreign country.

'I'm sorry I wasn't much company,' she told the man who'd driven her as they left his car in a long-term car park—talk about positive thinking!—and walked towards the airport building.

'You have travelled far,' he said, understanding in his voice.

Inside the terminal, they found the rest of the party easily, for all were wearing, over their shirts, white singlets with the distinctive red cross of the organisation across the chest and back.

'Here's one for each of you,' the team leader said, introducing himself as Martin Yorke, an English doctor who had worked for many years in the country and was now returning in the hope of helping people he thought of as his friends.

The rest of the team, when Rachel had been introduced and had woken up enough to sort out who was who, were technical people, drafted to help get essential services working again. Phone technicians, pumping experts, mechanics and structural engineers—all would have a role to play in helping the country back to stability.

What surprised Rachel most was the enthusiasm they all showed, as if they were off on an exciting adventure.

But twenty-four hours later the enthusiasm had waned considerably. They had been bumping along in the back of an old van for what seemed like for ever. Dust seeped through the canvas sides and every jolt on the road hurt the bruises they were all carrying.

'Not as bad as East Africa,' one of the men said, and talk turned to other places these volunteers had served. And as she listened, Rachel felt her own enthusiasm returning, her doubts about what lay ahead—what would Luca think of her arriving?—set aside as she contemplated how, if things didn't work out with him, she could make a new life for herself on missions such as this.

They crawled into the capital at dawn, the vehicle stopping first at the hospital as most of the supplies were medical.

Now the doubts returned, and with them fear that Luca might not still be there. Might not even be alive…

'He will be all right,' the doctor who'd driven her to Switzerland assured her, and Rachel frowned at him. Now virtual strangers were reading her face!

The hospital, though the corridors were crammed with patients, smelt and felt like hospitals did all over the world, the familiarity helping soothe Rachel's agitation. Martin spoke the language and it was he who asked for news of Luca.

A long, involved conversation followed, accompanied by much waving of arms.

'He's here, in a ward at the end of this corridor,' Martin said at last, then he hesitated, shrugged his shoulders and added, 'But if you could see him really quickly, this man was telling me they're about to operate on a child who's had the bottom part of both legs blown off and they have no theatre staff. We'll need you there.'

Luca was at the end of the corridor, but a child who'd been very badly injured was in Theatre?

'Let's go straight to Theatre,' she said to Martin. 'Some of those boxes have theatre instruments in them. Shall we carry them through with us? These people are busy enough handling their patients without having to lug boxes.'

Martin beamed at her, then spoke to the man again.

'I have told him to let Luca know you are here,' he said, following her back towards the old truck.

'You wouldn't believe where the shrapnel's got to,'

Martin said, an hour later. He had tied off blood vessels and neatened the stumps of the child's legs, but during the operation the patient's blood pressure had dropped so low, the makeshift team of Martin, Rachel and a local nurse, doing the anaesthetic, had realised there was something else seriously wrong.

The child had stood on a land-mine, but as well as the immediate damage to his legs, shrapnel from the blast had pierced his bowel and all but severed his inferior mesenteric artery. Now, with the artery fixed and the damage to the bowel removed, Martin was searching for missing pieces of metal, afraid that if he missed one, all the work they'd already done to save the boy's life would go to waste.

'There!' Rachel said, spotting a piece close to one kidney.

'It wouldn't be so bad if we could be sure they'd stay where they are,' Martin grumbled, 'but if they start moving around the abdominal cavity and one pierces the bowel again or, heaven forbid, the kid's heart, he'll be in trouble.'

Rachel used saline to flush out the abdomen again and again but, conscious of limited supplies, she didn't flood the cavity but drew the fluid into a syringe and squirted it around.

The operating table was low, and her back ached, while tiredness from too much travel and not enough sleep tightened all the muscles in her shoulders and neck so even the slightest movement was agony.

Then the tension eased, as if someone had wiped a magic cloth across her shoulders. Wonderingly, she raised her head and looked around.

Luca stood just inside the room, a mask held across his mouth and nose, his eyes feasting on her—his face, for once, as easy for her to read as he found hers. For amazement, disbelief and, most of all, love were all reflected in his eyes. She knew he smiled behind the mask before he shook his head and left again.

The young local who was doing the anaesthetic spoke to Martin, his voice excited and emphatic.

'Seems your boyfriend has been all but running the hospital, operating day and night, never sleeping, teaching people to take care of their sick and injured relatives, performing minor miracles right, left and centre,' Martin explained.

And although she couldn't see his mouth, Rachel knew he, too, was smiling, and the warmth of the love she felt for Luca spread through her body, banishing pain and stiffness—even banishing her doubts...

CHAPTER ELEVEN

THEY caught snatched moments together over the next few days, but time only to hold each other, not to talk. Well, not to talk much, though Luca had scolded her for coming, and called her a fool and idiot, but in a voice so filled with love Rachel knew he didn't mean it.

He was exhausted, and Martin, who was now nominally in charge of the hospital, had ordered him to bed soon after the arrival of the reinforcements.

Then Rachel was asleep while Luca woke up and returned to work, and it seemed as if their schedule would never allow them the time they needed together.

But apart from that frustration, which Rachel was too busy to let bother her, there was so much to be thankful for.

She was close to Luca for a start, and she could feel his love whenever he was near. On top of that, the baby was doing well, already off the ventilator, and surprisingly healthy in spite of lack of the personal care and attention he'd have received in a PICU. A young aide, following orders from Luca, was with him a lot of the time, nursing not only the post-op patient but other babies in the small ward.

Rachel learned her way around the single-storied building, built as a hollow square around a garden, spending time in Theatre when she was needed, helping out on the wards when no operations were under way. She learned a few words of the local language, and became friends with the local staff, finding them all gentle people, as bemused and distressed by what was happening in their country as people in any war-torn place must be.

Luca found her in the garden with the little boy who'd lost his legs, teaching him nursery rhymes from her own childhood. For a long time he just looked at her, taking in the dusty jeans and grubby T-shirt, the once shiny hair dulled by dust and lack of time to wash it, her face alight with pleasure as the little boy repeated words he didn't understand after her.

That she had come to find him still seemed unbelievable, and, though his initial reaction had been anger that she'd put herself in danger, now his heart was so full of happiness he didn't think he'd ever be able to express it.

He walked towards her, to tell her some news Martin had just imparted. The airfield had been cleared and more medical people were flying in the following day. They could fly out on the plane bringing in the relief later tomorrow.

He knew he must be frowning and tried to wipe the expression off his face, knowing Rachel would pick up on it.

'Luca!'

She looked up at him and breathed his name. Nothing more, just that, but the word was so full of love he thought his heart would burst.

'I love you,' he said, knowing the words had to be in English this time. Then he knelt beside her and took her hand. 'Always and for ever.'

She looked at him, her amber eyes as serious as he

had ever seen them, then a sad little smile tilted up the left side of her lips.

'That sounds a lot like the little speech you made back in the lounge at Jimmie's when I yelled at you and then you headed off to be captured by rebels in a foreign country.'

'I meant it then and I mean it now. Yes, I *had* thought of you coming to work for me, with me—of the two of us working together—but that was an added attraction quite apart from my love, because first and always it was you.'

Then his mouth dried up and no more words would come. She looked at him, eyes wide, the little boy on her knee also watching him.

'There's more, isn't there?' she whispered, the sad smile back in place.

He took her hands and nodded.

'A relief team is flying in tomorrow and the Red Cross has promised more medical staff to follow. Martin has suggested we fly out on tomorrow's plane when it leaves. He says we'll no longer be needed here.'

He hesitated, then said, 'I would like you on that plane. Away from this place.'

'But you said *we'll* no longer be needed—that means both of us, Luca.'

'I would go, but I cannot leave the baby. I know I haven't been able to spend much time with him, neither can I do anything any competent nurse couldn't do, but his drug regimen is still too important to his survival to leave him unsupervised.' He met her eyes and she knew he was begging her to understand.

'I can't leave so fragile a patient without specialist care.'

Rachel heard the words, and deep inside she felt them as well. This was part of what she loved about this man—his commitment to the infants he served.

Although…

'But he is one baby, Luca. Back in Italy there are dozens of babies who would benefit from your skills. Don't they need you, too?'

'There are other specialists back there,' he reminded her. 'And I don't intend staying for ever— just until we know the little boy is stable, and the hospital is operating efficiently enough for me to know he will get proper treatment. You understand?'

Understanding was one thing, but to leave this place without Luca?

It was unthinkable.

'We could take him with us,' Rachel suggested. 'He's off the ventilator, but even if he needed oxygen, there'd be some way we could hook him up to the plane's supply.'

'Take him with us?'

He looked so startled Rachel had to smile.

'Think about it, Luca. He'll need a second op before too long and, no matter how long you stay, you don't have the facilities to do it here. As things are, his parents aren't seeing him at all, but if we could visit them, or get a message to them, and suggest we do this, then, when things settle down here and they're free to travel—

'*If* they're free to travel!'

Rachel shrugged off the interruption.

'Whatever! They'll either be reunited with him or they won't, but at least the little boy will be OK. Don't you think they'd choose life for him no matter what their fate? They made that choice, travelling to Australia with him for the operation.'

Luca still looked bemused, though now he was frowning.

'But someone will have to care for him. He won't be in hospital for ever.'

'*I'll* care for him,' Rachel said quietly, hugging the little boy on her lap a little closer. 'I know he won't be mine but that won't stop me loving him, and I'll go into it knowing it's a foster-situation and one day I'll have to give him back. But I could do it, Luca. I *would* do it.'

She swallowed the lump in her throat and looked at him, not wanting to beg for his agreement but silently beseeching him to see her point. Then he smiled and she knew everything would be all right.

'*We* could do it,' he said softly, then he leaned forward and kissed her on the cheek. 'But you are sure? You would take on this child, knowing of his problems? Knowing you could grow to love him then lose him, one way or another?'

Rachel knew how important the question was, and she paused, thinking it through, before she answered.

'I'm sure, Luca.'

He must have heard the certainty in her voice for he nodded.

'I'll go and see who I can sweet-talk into letting me contact the parents.'

Rachel caught his hand.

'Go carefully,' she whispered. 'Don't put yourself in danger again.'

Luca touched his palm to her cheek.

'I won't do that—but I've built up some credibility

working here, and I think I know who to approach about this.'

Another kiss and he was gone, leaving Rachel half excited and half anxious. No matter how much work Luca had done for injured rebel soldiers in the hospital, if he was seen to be aligning himself with the old regime he could end up in trouble.

She didn't see him again until late that night. She was sitting by the baby's bed, wondering about his future, when she heard footsteps coming along the aisle between the beds.

Luca's footsteps, she was sure, though if she'd been asked if she could recognise them she'd have said no.

She turned to see him, and even in the muted light of the ward, she could see the smile on his face.

Behind him, two other figures moved, but it wasn't until Luca introduced them that Rachel realised his sweet-talking had achieved a miracle—the baby's parents had been released and would fly to Switzerland with the departing aid workers.

'So we shall all go,' Luca whispered, drawing Rachel away so the parents could touch their son.

Luca's arms closed around her and he held her for a minute, neither of them speaking—content just to be together.

'Come, I'll walk you to your room,' he whispered, and the huskiness in his voice told her just where that walk would lead. But much as she wanted to lie in Luca's arms and forget, for a little while, the horrors she had witnessed, she had to shake her head.

'One last night—I promised Martin I'd stay on duty. I can sleep when we're finally on the plane.'

Luca's arms tightened around her and he kissed the

top of her head—thank heavens she'd scrounged that bucket of water and washed her hair today!

'And I promised Martin I'd see some of the new patients that were brought in from some outlying district where fighting continues,' Luca admitted. 'But once we're home, my lovely Rachel, we will shut ourselves away in my apartment and make up for lost time.'

But Luca was wrong. Once home, he was claimed first by media people demanding interviews and information, then by government people demanding more information, then by his family, who clustered protectively around him, talking, hugging, touching him as if to make sure he was really there.

And through most of it, Rachel slept. They were staying at Paola's as the paparazzi were camped outside Luca's apartment building. Paola had taken one look at Rachel and led her to a bathroom, insisting she take as long as she like in the shower, handing her a towelling robe to put on after it, and showing her a bedroom near the bathroom where she could sleep.

'You are still sleeping?'

Luca's voice—the bed moving—Luca's body sliding in beside hers, smelling fresh and clean and so masculine Rachel felt excitement stir within her.

'Not now,' she whispered, but though he put his arms around her and drew her close, he was asleep before the kiss he brushed against her lips was finished.

So now he slept, while she watched over him, content to have him near while she explored all the wondrous feelings that were tied up in her love for Luca.

EPILOGUE

THE summer sun beat down on the pavement, drawing up swirls of steamy heat.

'We could have called a cab,' Luca complained as he walked from the apartment to the hospital with his wife of three months.

'But that wouldn't have been the same,' Rachel told him, clinging to his arm and thinking of the other times they'd walked together along this pavement.

Luca had wanted to stay in a hotel in the city for this short trip back to Sydney, but Rachel had begged him to try to get his old apartment back, or another one in the same building.

'Not to relive the past,' she'd said, 'but for the fun of it.'

So here they were, walking the familiar street, Rachel excited at the prospect of seeing her friends again, though Kurt, Alex and Annie, and Phil and Maggie had all flown to Italy to celebrate Luca and Rachel's wedding.

As they reached the hospital gates, they saw Kurt standing there, while the other two couples were approaching from the opposite direction.

Kurt kissed Rachel on the cheek, shook hands with Luca, then put his arm around Rachel in his usual proprietorial way.

'That guy treating you OK?' he asked, and Luca saw colour sweep into Rachel's cheeks.

So often in this way she showed him her thoughts

of love, but this time, he suspected, the colour was due to other thoughts. Thoughts of the baby they had just learned she was carrying.

Maggie, too, was pregnant, and having discovered she had a luteal phase defect, which had caused her previous miscarriages, daily injections during her early pregnancy had ensured she would carry this baby to full term.

Luca wondered if Phil felt the same ridiculously overwhelming pride in Maggie's pregnancy that he himself was feeling in Rachel's. His sisters were constantly teasing him about the perpetual smile on his face, but why wouldn't he be smiling when he had so much to be happy about?

He looked at the woman who'd brought him this happiness. She was talking to Kurt, asking him about his life and his decision to remain in Australia when the rest of the team returned to the US.

Asking him even more personal questions, if the colour now rising in *Kurt's* cheeks was any indication.

Luca smiled to himself. Rachel had been certain her friend must finally have found someone he really loved, hence the decision to remain in Sydney as part of the new team at Jimmie's.

She was also hoping to meet this 'someone' during their few days in Sydney, and was no doubt pestering Kurt about where and when this meeting could take place.

Then the others reached them, and after a flurry of kisses, hugs and handshakes they walked as a group into the hospital grounds, where a big marquee had been set up for the official opening ceremony of the

St James's Children's Hospital Paediatric Cardiac Surgical Unit.

Becky was waiting for them inside, ready to usher them into their places in the front row of seats.

'And how's my favourite sexy Italian?' she whispered to Luca.

'Very well,' he told her formally, then nodded to where Ned hovered not far away. 'And how are you?' he teased, knowing an engagement between the couple was imminent.

'So happy I could shout it to the stars,' Becky said, and Lùca knew exactly what she meant.

He put his arm around his wife and guided her to her seat, then, as he had done on the bus many months ago, he held her hand.

She was smiling, but he knew she was sad inside, for this was the real end of the team she, Kurt and Alex had been for many years. And this was the real goodbye to her friends, although Luca was sure they would all see each other whenever possible.

Then she leaned closer to him and whispered in his ear.

'I loved my work, but not nearly as much as I love you,' she reminded him, and he wondered when she'd begun to read his thoughts!

A dais had been erected in the front of the marquee, and above it the name of the new unit had been printed on a very long banner.

'At least no one will be able to make an acronym of it,' Kurt said. 'I mean, how would you pronounce SJCHPCSU?'

'Maybe they could call it Jimmie's kids' hearts' unit,' Maggie suggested.

'Or just,' Annie said quietly, ''A Very Special Place''. Wouldn't that describe it?'

And the people who'd worked to establish the unit, and save the lives of children who'd come through its doors, all nodded their agreement.

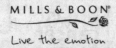

researching the cure

The facts you need to know:

- **One woman in nine** in the United Kingdom will develop breast cancer during her lifetime.

- Each year **40,700** women are newly diagnosed with breast cancer and around **12,800** women will die from the disease. However, survival rates are improving, with on average 77 per cent of women still alive five years later.

- **Men can also suffer from breast cancer**, although currently they make up less than one per cent of all new cases of the disease.

Britain has one of the highest breast cancer death rates in the world. Breast Cancer Campaign wants to understand why and do something about it. Statistics cannot begin to describe the impact that breast cancer has on the lives of those women who are affected by it and on their families and friends.

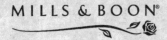

MILLS & BOON®

During the month of October Harlequin Mills & Boon will donate 10p from the sale of every Modern Romance™ series book to help Breast Cancer Campaign in *researching the cure*.

Breast Cancer Campaign's scientific projects look at improving diagnosis and treatment of breast cancer, better understanding how it develops and ultimately either curing the disease or preventing it.

Do your part to help

Visit <u>www.breastcancercampaign.org</u>

And make a donation today.

researching the cure

Breast Cancer Campaign is a company limited by guarantee registered in England and Wales. Company No. 05074725. Charity registration No. 299758.

FREE!

4 Books
and a surprise gift!

We would like to take this opportunity to thank you for reading this Mills & Boon® book by offering you the chance to take FOUR more specially selected titles from the Medical Romance™ series absolutely FREE! We're also making this offer to introduce you to the benefits of the Reader Service™—

- ★ **FREE home delivery**
- ★ **FREE gifts and competitions**
- ★ **FREE monthly Newsletter**
- ★ **Exclusive Reader Service offers**
- ★ **Books available before they're in the shops**

Accepting these FREE books and gift places you under no obligation to buy, you may cancel at any time, even after receiving your free shipment. Simply complete your details below and return the entire page to the address below. You don't even need a stamp!

YES! Please send me 4 free Medical Romance books and a surprise gift. I understand that unless you hear from me, I will receive 6 superb new titles every month for just £2.75 each, postage and packing free. I am under no obligation to purchase any books and may cancel my subscription at any time. The free books and gift will be mine to keep in any case.

M5ZEF

Ms/Mrs/Miss/Mr ....Initials ....
Surname .... BLOCK CAPITALS PLEASE
Address ....

....
....Postcode ....

Send this whole page to:
UK: FREEPOST CN81, Croydon, CR9 3WZ

PRAISE FOR CARLENE THOMPSON

"Thompson creates smart, interesting characters the reader cares about within a gripping suspense story."
—Judith Kelman, author of *After the Fall* on *Don't Close Your Eyes*

BLACK FOR REMEMBRANCE

"Gripped me from the first page and held on through its completely unexpected climax. Lock your doors, make sure there's no one behind you, and pick up *Black for Remembrance*."
—William Katz, author of *Double Wedding*

"Bizarre, terrifying...an inventive and forceful psychological thriller."
—*Publishers Weekly*

SINCE YOU'VE BEEN GONE

"This story will keep readers up well into the night."
—*Huntress Reviews*

DON'T CLOSE YOUR EYES

"*Don't Close Your Eyes* has all the gothic sensibilities of a Victoria Holt novel, combined with the riveting modern suspense of Sharyn McCrumb's *The Hangman's Beautiful Daughter*. Don't close your eyes—and don't miss this one."
—Meagan McKinney, author of *In the Dark*

"*Don't Close Your Eyes* is an exciting romantic suspense novel that will thrill readers with the subplots of a who-done-it and a legendary resident ghost seen only by children...The reviewer suggests finishing this terrific tale in one sitting to ascertain how accurate are the reader's deductive skills in pinpointing the true villain."
—Harriet Klausner

IN THE EVENT OF MY DEATH

"[A] blood-chilling...tale of vengeance, madness, and murder."
—*Romantic Times*

THE WAY YOU LOOK TONIGHT

"Thompson...has crafted a lively, entertaining read...skillfully ratchet[ing] up the tension with each successive chapter."
—*The Charleston Daily Mail*

ST. MARTIN'S PAPERBACKS TITLES
BY CARLENE THOMPSON